Tomorrow
or
Forever

TRANSGRESS·PRESS

TOMORROW
OR
FOREVER

Stories

JACK KAULFUS

For my mother, Sue Kaulfus

Contents

Cibola

THE PLANE WAS supposed to land in Vancouver. When the cabin door opened, Martin noted with some degree of dismay that the air creeping inside was sticky and moist. He hastily repacked his carry-on and shuffled down the main aisle with the others. Outside, the passengers were quiet and calm, leisurely unscrewing the tops of their soda bottles while they waited for further direction. A circle of high school basketball players didn't even unplug themselves from their phones. The crew stood in a line, their faces prettily blank.

"We're absolutely fine, sir. Safe and sound." The same flight attendant who had poured him a Diet Coke over ice only twenty minutes before now mildly suggested that Martin gather his luggage from the cargo storage in the belly of the plane.

"But this isn't Vancouver," Martin said.

"That's right," the flight attendant said agreeably. He pointed past Martin to the bags being dropped at the feet of waiting passengers. Martin found his suitcase among all the others and wheeled it over to a despondent looking Frances, who was poking at her phone.

"No signal," she said, as Martin approached. "Where the fuck are we?"

There was no airport in sight; no building, in fact, anywhere. They were surrounded on all sides by watery ferns and soft mossy tree trunks. Martin couldn't tell how the plane had even landed in such a small area, unless the runway was hidden away somewhere in the greenery. He stood his suitcase upright and turned to ask a passing woman what she knew. The woman smiled vaguely and pulled her messenger bag over her head. She glanced down at her own phone.

"Layover?" she ventured. Martin felt around in his breast pocket for his ticket and boarding pass, and remembered he'd pushed them into the seat pocket in front of him and forgotten about them. A cool wind hit his face; he caught a whiff of rain.

"Layover, where?" he asked the woman. She seemed dazed.

She shrugged and looked around. "Maybe not. Maybe this is Vancouver."

Frances pulled on Martin's sleeve. "Look around," she said. "I told you. No baby."

Beyond the plane, a line of folks followed a flight attendant toward a corner of the cracked tarmac.

"Come on," he said. Frances heaved her bag onto her shoulder and they left the plane and its stoppered occupants behind. Before they'd reached the edge of the tarmac, the rain was coming down hard. Martin took his glasses off. He could just make out a blurry path through the brush where the others had disappeared. Frances found his hand and pulled him into the darkness.

He hadn't been sure about the trip at first – given his daughter's unsettled sleeping patterns and his wife's recent reluctance to speak plainly with him about anything but groceries. Once he got inside the taxi, though, and let his thoughts begin to settle back into their own natural rhythm, he began to look forward to some time alone. Outside his window, the autumn afternoon was gray and gold. He decided he loved November. Then, he loved the airport. The books everywhere, the people in too-warm jackets, the sound of waiting planes. He shut off his phone early and decided not to turn it on again until his feet were on solid pavement in Vancouver.

His plane was about half full. Martin tried not to let disappointment register on his face when a young woman paused next to him to examine her ticket. When Martin made a move to get up, she told him not to bother. She crawled over him and settled into the window seat, smashing her bag down between her feet. She gave him a quick smile, much the way his shier students from the back row acknowledged him when they saw him standing in line at Fat Burger like a regular person. Her hair was short. There was a small silver ball surfing the barrel of her bottom lip; a matching chain sitting snug against her neck.

She fished her phone from the pocket of her black hooded sweatshirt and began texting. Martin directed the air spigot at the top of his head and opened his book to pretend to read while he watched her thumbs hover over the keypad.

Even though he'd chosen carefully, he wasn't interested in his mystery. He closed it and half-listened to the speech about emergency exits. The bored flight attendant showing them how to work the oxygen masks filled out her AirTrack uniform like an elegant linebacker. She pointed at the floor, the ceiling, the exits, her own eyes following her hands. Martin thought about what it would feel like to perform every day to such an indifferent audience. The young woman next to him shut her phone off and slipped it into a pocket of the bag at her feet. She glanced at him.

"Emergency Exit, Row 12," she said, leaning over to tap the door in front of them.

Martin retrieved his boarding pass from the pocket of his shirt, wondering if she thought him incapable of handling an emergency. He studied the pass down beside his knee. The past few months, words and numbers less than an arm's length away had become difficult to see without his glasses.

"Are you prepared for the worst?" she asked brightly.

Martin nodded. "You?"

She shrugged. "Don't know. But I'm liking the leg room."

The plane taxied for almost fifteen minutes, during which time the young woman retrieved her cell phone and sent another text. This time, Martin only caught the second half: *Open the drawer near table and look under scarf.*

She caught him looking. "Spy," she said.

"I'm sure it's just my age," Martin said, "but for me, one of the great things about planes is that nobody expects me to be available." He offered the young woman a piece of gum to protect her ears against the sudden pressure in the cabin. "Don't people know you're on a plane?"

The young woman put the gum in her mouth and tightened her seatbelt as the engines came to life. "None of your business," she said.

Fair enough, Martin thought. He settled back into his seat, considering mildly that the conversation he just had could have been his last. The plane lifted, swung wildly to the left. Martin felt his heart quicken as he raised his eyes to the window, but the plane righted itself and all he could see were the checkerboard fields disappearing smoothly beneath the plane. Something like disappointment settled in his chest.

It wasn't a death wish, exactly, he told himself. It wasn't. He was, perhaps, simply prematurely preoccupied with the next thing. He couldn't be sure what the next thing might be. For now, he understood he was loved, though maybe somewhat painfully, by his daughter and his unhappy wife. He knew this was lucky. He watched his cholesterol and wore a seat belt. But death, perhaps an accident or the sudden end of an organ's life—the moment, then the afterward—was a private, desperate yearning that pulled at the edges of his days. It didn't worry him anymore, really. Upon uncovering this predilection as a teen, he'd immediately recognized the need to protect himself against the shifty desires of his subconscious—in case his limbs got together one day and decided to throw Martin off the Talk Box at the top of the school stadium. He designated himself the sober driver for his baseball team, sometimes dodging punches while prying keys from drunken fists.

And now, these thoughts were locked securely away behind the doors of obligation. Martin was sometimes grateful for the weight of his daughter's routine, grateful for the distraction. Without it, he sensed there would surely be a kind of untethering beginning at his feet and ending at the top of his head. He'd rise like Gulliver. He'd float like a weather balloon. He'd burn like the Hindenburg.

He opened his book to a page about three quarters in. Maybe it got better. Within a few minutes, the young woman beside him was fast asleep, phone in hand. Her head lolled first against the curve of the window and then gently against her flat chest. In this state, she looked a bit older than he first guessed. She reminded him of his daughter, only older. A bit of hair, longer in the front than the back, fell over her right eye. He wondered if this is how Kelly would look in fifteen years—unafraid, distinctly unfeminine, caught in a state of semi-permanent adolescence.

This was closer than he'd been to anyone outside his family in years. He listened to her breathing, strangely moved by the rhythm, while her phone vibrated in her lap and then clattered to the floor of the plane.

Martin was headed to Vancouver for an art education conference, the only one that year his school had agreed to pay for. It was a stupid conference, actually, the panels promising to teach him technology he'd never be savvy enough use into his classroom. He hoped for cold rain, thick cloud cover, maybe other reasons to stay inside. He planned to spend most of his time drinking coffee and looking out on the Vancouver streets. Martin's wife had told him to use the time to reconsider their relationship.

"I want you to know I've been thinking about your future," she'd told him, handing him the beard trimmer she'd picked up for the trip. He'd had his eye on it for some time. When she began her sentences with *I want you to know* he was always thrown off by the immediate promise of intimacy. Even after so many years, he could not tell when she would deliver.

"What about it?" he'd asked, stabbing ineffectively at the hard plastic with his pocket knife.

"I think you should think about going back to school. Remember that offer you got from Will? I think you should drop him a line."

His old friend Will owned a gallery in Dallas. He hadn't spoken to Will in two years.

"What are you talking about?" Martin asked.

Sarah shrugged. Lately, her face had begun to remind him of a leaky balloon. "Kelly's getting to be self-sufficient. Pretty soon, she'll be asking us if we can afford out of state tuition."

"She's twelve." Martin folded back the straight blade on the trimmer and plugged it in.

"Exactly."

It was a setup. A few minutes into the discussion, it became clear that Sarah wanted Martin to consider going back to school so he could support himself when she left. The fancy beard trimmer, now charging on the dresser, seemed suddenly suspect. Maybe Sarah was already dating.

MARTIN LEANED OVER and dug around. Her phone was so small it fit snugly in the palm of his hand. He meant to simply silence it, but at his touch the screen sprang into a festival of treetops. Martin cupped his other hand over the screen. When he uncovered it again, the trees had been replaced by a list of names beginning with A. Before he could think, he scrolled down to M and pressed the call button on his own name. He imagined himself at his desk at home on any other Friday afternoon, flipping open his phone, lowering his voice just a little to greet the caller.

"Hello, Martin?"

"Plane's going down."

"Martin?"

He shut the phone down while it was still ringing on the other end and gently pushed it into the seat pocket in front of her. The flight attendants were pushing the drink cart down the aisle.

THE YOUNG WOMAN awoke with a start, her eyes fixed wide on the upright tray in front of her, as if it held the last scene of her dream. He'd witnessed a similar expression on Kelly, who refused to awaken from night terrors even when removed from her bed. Delicate, iron willed Kelly, who never believed their stories the next morning.

"No, I dreamed about horses," she'd told Martin over her bagel and jelly just the day before Martin's trip. Sarah had been up three solid hours in the middle of the night, arms wrapped tightly around her struggling daughter. Martin had come in during that third hour, a cup of warm milk in hand for his wife, to find her in tears. Kelly's back was arched, her face caving in on itself.

"You don't recall doing any screaming?" Martin asked his daughter, pouring her a glass of juice.

"Maybe when we were running really fast," she said. "Maybe on the beach." Sarah raised her eyebrows. A warning. She looked leakier than usual. Martin wondered briefly if what he was feeling for her was love, still. He decided it didn't matter until he returned from Vancouver.

He was glad Kelly didn't remember, but he couldn't help wonder what she buried and carried into the day—what loathsome images might flash before the long division on the chalkboard, what misplaced dread might hang over the stalls in the girl's bathroom. "You're awake just in time," Martin said to the young woman, keeping his voice even and low. "Here come the drinks." She dropped her head into her hands and rubbed her eyes. Up ahead, a baby let out a wail.

"You want a water or something?" he asked the young woman, accepting his own little cup of diet coke from a young beautiful flight attendant with a wide brown forehead. The girl looked up, remnants of the dream still playing across the space between her eyes. She nodded and accepted a sealed bottle, which she slipped into the bag at her feet. She turned her face back toward the window.

"You all right?" Martin asked.

"No." The girl faced him, suddenly. "You know where we are?"

Martin laughed. "In the air?"

The girl shook her head. "I don't think we're going the right way."

Martin leaned past the girl and looked out the window. They were at cruising altitude, on the shadow side of the sunset. "Which way do you think we're going?"

The girl followed his gaze. "Jesus, I don't know," she said. She sighed, tiredly. "I just got this feeling. I had this dream or something."

Martin offered his hand. "Look, I'm Martin. I can't manage maps on the *ground*, so up here, I'm kind of at the mercy of the pilot."

The girl nodded. Her face oriented a little. "I guess I'm a little stressed. My sister just moved out to the country with her boyfriend and he took off. She's a mess."

"You're going for a visit?"

She smiled. "I don't know I'm that much better off, though." She took Martin's hand. "Frances."

"I've got a conference," Martin said. He felt a little loose. In a mock-secret whisper, he told Frances he was planning to register at the conference and then disappear into the city.

"Ever been?" she asked.

"Never been outside the U.S."

"I hope you like trees."

The crying baby gained momentum a couple of rows in front of them. Frances unbuckled her belt and stood. She excused herself, squeezed past Martin, and walked up the aisle. The nose of the plane dipped dramatically, and Martin was acutely aware of his ear canals. Frances paused briefly and looked around. Hanging on to the seatbacks, she propelled herself toward Martin again as the plane lurched.

Martin leaned back to let her back into her seat, but she only leaned over and whispered: "Something's not right." Her thick silver necklace hung very near his chin.

"What? Is the baby sick or something?" Martin wished she'd sit down again. He pointed at the lit seatbelt sign.

Frances shook her head. "There's no baby."

"Well, there *is* a baby, because the baby is crying." He realized he was using the Patient Voice of Reason his students and daughter hated—especially when they were on the edge of a freak-out. "Why don't you have a seat?" Martin patted the combination air-flotation device and cushion beside him.

"There's no baby, Martin."

"I hear the baby, Frances."

"No shit. But I always ask the desk attendants if any kids under two will be on board. I fucking hate babies on planes. You know? They cry. They cry like *this*." Frances spread her hands and looked behind her, as if the baby might make a sudden appearance. "But I just checked. No baby."

"I'm sure you're mistaken," Martin said, though he found himself unbuckling his own belt and rising for a quick site check. The baby's cries were growing steadily more insistent. Martin felt a familiar wobbling anger rising in the back of his throat. He pushed it down again, willing it away. It was the kind of anger, threatening and focused, that had forced him out of the house and into the backyard while Kelly screamed through her third colicky month of life—an anger that was only mediated by space, and only melted by twenty guilty minutes of chain-smoking. As Kelly grew older, Martin thought he'd be relieved to find himself only infrequently reminded of this anger, happy to let it slide into the annals of bygone parenting stressors, along with early morning pee sheets.

It only got harder. The wobble never fully disappeared. The angry confusion of fatherhood never quite left his mind, much like the not-quite-death wish. He never fully got used to the discomfort of role-modeling every second of his life. Of pretending to care about the state of the yard, or the state of his hair, even, because good fathers *show*. They don't just say. They show.

Kelly had announced just the week before that she wasn't meant to grow up to be woman after all. She had decided, after all their careful social grooming and feminist diatribe, that she was to be a man. She had decided, in all her stubborn sadness, that she was not who she was. She announced she would no longer be shopping in the Misses section. Immediately, she began taking up new space with her knobby little body. How he was supposed to usher his little girl into the ways of manhood, he had no idea.

It should not have been such a surprise. Her third year on earth, she was telling strangers to stop using "she." The year she was seven, Kelly's favorite book was an illustrated account of Francisco Coronado's failed expedition to find the fabled Seven Cities of Cibola. Martin had rescued it from the free bin outside the library. The pictures intrigued him: crude four-color panel pastels, blue, red, black and yellow— Coronado himself a mere slip of a man in flowering trousers. The most substantial thing about him was his helmet: yellow as the city of his dreams.

Kelly scoured the house and fashioned a Coronado costume from pieces of her old roman soldier Halloween costume and a skirt of Sarah's, stolen from the hamper. She insisted that her friends and family refer to her as "Conquistador," having realized much earlier she could not break any of them of the habit of using feminine pronouns alongside her name. She spent much of her time at home crashing through the banana trees in the backyard in search of a glittering, golden Quivira. Martin would be watching television while Kelly snuck through the den as though she'd never seen it before, eyeing Martin as though he might be a Zuni warrior, relaxing with a bit of human sacrifice and a beer.

Later, Sarah confiscated the book and replaced it with a prettier one that took the savage nature of the American Indian and spread it to the rest of the human race. Typhoid-infested blankets and firearms, things like that. Kelly hated it. She claimed, years later, to still be searching used bookstores for her beloved, racist tome. She was still coming up empty-handed.

A SLIM, DARK haired flight attendant appeared behind Frances and asked her to take her seat. Frances obliged, begrudgingly.

"I wish you could still smoke on these planes," he said. "You used to be able to *buy* cigarettes from the flight attendants."

Frances looked at him. "If something happens to me," she said, "will you call my family?" She pressed a business card into his hand.

Martin laughed. "Are you serious?"

"Serious as the invisible baby."

Out the window, plumes of dusky cloud were breaking up over the wing. They were not cruising anymore.

FRANCES'S HAND WAS sure and strong. Martin followed her down the path and through the doors of a hotel on a hill that overlooked many miles of lakes and trees and possibly the rocky coastline in the far distance. The hotel seemed an upscale Marriot or similar, though Martin didn't see any branding around the lobby.

The front desk stretched the length of the lobby and was staffed by lovely, trim folks in khaki-colored scrubs. Martin stepped up beside Frances while she checked in, not sure whether he was sticking close by for her sake or his.

"Put your credit cards away," assured the woman behind the front desk. "Your stay's on us."

"When do we depart again for Vancouver?" Frances asked.

"Oh, they'll keep you updated on your progress," the woman said. "You'll want to come to the dining room before nine o'clock tonight for your first briefing." She handed Frances a key-card and turned to

Martin. "Now, Sir, we can put you and your daughter in adjoining rooms."

Martin turned to Frances. "We aren't—"

"That's great," Frances said, shouldering past Martin to the stack of bags just wheeled in from the rain. Martin got his key card and bag and they found the elevator bank, which must have housed twenty-five separate shafts on each side of the hallway. Martin's room had no television, no phone, but he could hear a canned voice, maybe a radio, down the hall. The walls were plain, cinderblock freshly painted over. Faint rainbows flickered here and there, as the light refracted through rivulets of rain on the window. He knocked on the door between his room and Frances's, and she opened it.

"This locks, by the way, in case you turn out to be a creep."

"I have a daughter back home," Martin assured.

"That means nothing to a creep," Frances said. "I'm going to rest up before dinner. You knock when you're ready go down, OK?" Martin agreed, and Frances locked the door between them.

Exhausted, he set his travel alarm for seven o'clock and fell asleep in his clothes on top of the hotel comforter. When he woke, he opened his luggage to find his creased jeans and sweaters gone, replaced with three white cotton jumpsuits. His toiletries, too, were missing. His beard trimmer. He decided he'd picked up the wrong luggage, and made a note to check in with the front desk downstairs.

The information given at the first briefing was sketchy, at best. At the front of the room, flight attendant Ella seemed less linebacker and more game-warden in a crisp safari outfit. Martin tried to listen, but Ella's microphone kept fading. There were about thirty people sitting in front of trays of food. Upon his plate sat an unappetizing attempt at a French Dip sandwich. To his left, Frances sipped black coffee.

"...may stay, free of charge, as long as you want," the microphone was in, then out again. "And you are free to walk away anytime you like. We don't provide transportation home, but we trust you will find your way when you are ready."

Frances raised her hand. "Walk away from what?"

"Your ideas matter," Ella went on. "After each briefing, you may choose to meet with a personal counselor to ask questions and share your thoughts. You can be sure we are listening to what you have to say."

Frances waved her hand again. "Where the fuck are we?"

Ella redirected her focus squarely upon Frances. "You want to leave?"

Frances nodded and glanced at Martin. Martin put his fork down. "I think we want to know how to get home. Or at least to Vancouver."

Ella put her hands in the mesh pockets of her khaki tunic and shrugged. "The door's open," she said.

It suddenly seemed absurd to Martin that they'd assumed they'd have to ask permission. He was thirty-eight years old. A U.S. citizen.

"Let's go," Frances said. She stood and turned around and addressed the crowd. "Anybody else?" A sea of faces turned away from her.

One woman met them at the back of the room, and the three of them filed out the open door. Martin followed Frances's blonde head, reaching out for her again the way he did when she pulled him into this mess. There were men in safari uniforms posted at each door down the hallway, but they only nodded as Martin and the others passed. "We're leaving," he told the men. Nobody tried to stop them.

The raindrops were heavy, but there were fewer of them. The sky, where he could make it out through the dense canopy, was the kind of white that suggested things might clear up soon. Martin, Frances, and the woman stopped beneath the branches of a wide and ancient looking pine about twenty feet from the entrance of the building.

"We gotta find that plane," Stephanie said, after introducing herself. She was tall and a bit unbalanced—her long legs seemed joined from the top of her thigh to her knee, opening into an "A" shape from knee to ankle.

"Can you *fly* a plane?" Frances asked her. Martin wished Frances could be a little more friendly, given their circumstances.

"You think they're just gonna let us walk out of here?" Stephanie turned toward Frances.

Martin squeezed Frances's shoulder before she could reply. "We don't even know where *here* is," he said. "Or who *they* are."

Stephanie shook her head. "I wasn't looking while we landed. But we were in the air about three hours. If we followed the flight plan, I think that might have put us somewhere near the border. Halfway?"

Martin hadn't been watching either—the baby wails had been deafening just before touchdown, and the usual announcements about seatbacks and tray tables hadn't been made.

"We didn't follow the flight plan, I'm sure of it," Frances said definitively. "Let's just explore. If we find the plane, at least maybe we can figure out how to call home."

The tarmac was empty. For the first time since landing, panic began to take hold. He took a deep breath, and on the exhale, spelled the names of his family waiting at home. Then he did it again. He glanced over his shoulder, memorizing the look of the route back to the hotel. This was something he did in parking lots by habit, after years of losing his car for years in rows and rows of anonymous headlights.

There was a path on the opposite side of the tarmac, so they followed it up a rocky incline, toward the sound of rushing water. They climbed steadily for a while, maybe an hour. Martin wasn't sure; his watch wasn't working anymore. The rain let up, and a warm, humid mist settled upon his skin like a blanket. Martin wished he had taken the lead; in front of him, Stephanie was limping, slowing down. He couldn't even see Frances any more as the path narrowed and leveled out ahead. Over the hill, he told himself, they'd get an idea of their whereabouts. Over the hill, they'd be able to see. Maybe get a drink.

Stephanie sat down on a rock just off the path on the right and pulled the leg of her jumpsuit up over her knee. It was swollen into a bluish baseball-sized knot. Martin knelt in front of her and touched the tight skin surrounding the patella. He called for Frances, but the water was like a wall of sound.

Stephanie shook her head, her eyes bright and slightly vacant. "I can keep going."

"You should elevate it," he told Stephanie, standing. "I'll come back when I see what's over the hill."

Stephanie shifted the bulk of her weight from the rock to the ground. Martin helped her get her calf up onto the rock. Her lips had stiffened into a dark line.

"I'll come back," Martin promised again.

"Just wait a minute. I'll be able to keep going."

Martin shook his head. He turned, leveraged his weight, and forced himself to keep going.

Now, as he neared the summit, as the sound of rushing water grew louder and louder in his ears, he found himself registering the crosshatched trees around him as seasonless, purposeless entities. The trunks didn't look any different from the ones nearer the tarmac, but he slowed and touched the bark of the nearest pine just to reassure himself. The tree was porous beneath his fingers, damp and soft, spongy. He pressed harder, and as he did, he caught a rhythm in the swollen, strident sound of the water—a skip on a looped recording. He withdrew his hand; his wet palm left an imprint that quickly filled again.

By the time he raised his face to the sky to call Frances's name, the clouds above him were darkening again. He was surprised at the sound of his own voice—the way it centered between his ears and stuck there. Maybe nothing was coming out of his mouth. Maybe it was all pointed inward. He looked down at his feet. The traction was off. When he willed himself to stop, the ground below him kept going a split second longer.

Martin forced his legs to move forward—not daring to look down at his feet again. When he glanced back over his shoulder to holler at Stephanie he knew before his eyes registered the absence that Stephanie would be gone. This path had been designed for Martin. It was his alone.

He was not surprised to be alone at the summit. He could see just fine: the trees and the blowing, white-tipped grass. Even under towering thunderheads, the city spread before him was bright as broken sunlight on a windy lake. It wasn't the kind of wall you could see or touch, but he knew he couldn't get down there. That place was at the end of a different path.

The sound of the water at the bottom of the hill below was hushed by the roar of a plane engine. Martin turned, only half expecting to see an AirTrack commuter lowering over the trees behind him. There was, of course, nothing.

Two DAYS LATER, the briefing rooms were full of shifting groups of people. Martin's hands, still raw from forcing his way back in through the window of his locked room, were giving him all kinds of hell. Once back in his room, he'd gone straight to the door of their adjoining rooms, hoping Frances had found her way back on her own. No one answered the door, but he could hear the canned voice a bit more clearly. He called her name, told her he wasn't a creep, that he wouldn't leave her again. He showered and tried to sleep: first naked, and then in one of the white jumpsuits. Every few minutes he knocked again for Frances.

More and more bands of people gathered at the back of every briefing and took off into the hallway. The word down the line was that four were too many. Two, too few. Martin pulled at the collar of his white jumpsuit, wondering what day it was back home. He looked around the room for Frances. At the afternoon briefing, he thought he'd caught a glimpse of her, only to lose her again in a crowd. She was still wearing the thick silver chain around her neck. That evening, he watched from the balcony overlooking the glassed yard, and her necklace glowed white in the diffused, falling light. It was comforting. He decided to wait to try a new path to the city. He wouldn't try to leave again without her.

The End of Objects

MIRELLE KNELT OVER a pile of blue sweaters and picked one that looked well-stitched. It was more used than others, but sturdily made. She had no way of knowing at which point it might be needed. Maybe it would be given to the girl at the beginning of a growth spurt, and she'd have to wear it through the winter even though it was too tight. Or maybe when the girl grew up to be a mother, she'd give it to her son; one of five sweaters wrapped by the maid under the tree on Christmas morning.

This was not the afterlife Mirelle had bargained for. She tossed the small sweater back onto the pile. Next to her, a blonde child laid four of them out for consideration. His bag was about half full. Mirelle wondered if he'd died young, or if he just felt like a seven–year-old. She'd noticed fewer gray hairs at her temples in the mirror and had a feeling she'd been rewound a decade or so. Before her body had begun its quiet, slow-moving rebellion.

"This is taking too long," he said, sitting back on his heels. "I just can't decide." His face was that of a child's—lightly freckled and delicate—but his voice was tense and old. Mirelle handed him a size 4T with a picture of a rocking horse sewn on the front. He turned it over in his hands for a few seconds, sighing, and handed it back.

"He's in, like, Alabama. These sweaters just mock him."

"Maybe if you go with a bigger one, there's a better chance he'll get more wear out of it. You know, statistically, we're adult-sized a lot longer than we're child-sized." Mirelle decided this was how she herself would choose, and she dug back in to find a generic looking size large. They watched a man kneel before the pile, grab a sweater, stuff it in his bag, and walk away.

"Careless," the boy said in a withering voice, turning his pink cheeks and pointed chin toward Mirelle. "But he can probably afford to be. Maybe he's got a whole envelope full of possibilities. What about you?"

"Oh, I think I'm going with this one—" Mirelle paused to open the envelope and slide the card out so he could see. "Female, controllable mental illness, no parents. America."

"Wow. No parents?"

Mirelle shook her head proudly. She felt pretty solid about the whole thing. Enough strife, enough safety net, and a familiar setting. The choice between the two had been easy. She wouldn't have had the first idea about how to prepare for the boy's complicated situation with his coach and the kinds of problems it might bring him. "I made it," Mirelle said. "She can make it."

HER PREDECESSOR HAD chosen for Mirelle a self-loathing, speed-addled mother, a philanderer of a father, and the body of a boy. Enough food, sure. Heat in the winter. But also a surprise gun barrel in her mouth one night after drinks with friends at the most popular gay club in Syracuse.

Tens of thousands of dollars in debt for necessary surgery to reverse the gender assigned at birth, she'd died at fifty-five after making a strong showing against lung cancer. She felt strangely indifferent about all the drama of life and death now. She'd been in love a few times, fostered dogs, been fired for dubious reasons, then employed as a case worker and counselor for AIDS survivors after returning to school for a license. She'd made a go of it, despite the absence of family that meant anything at all. After she died, they assured her at the gate that she'd done well.

"You didn't kill yourself or anyone else," said the woman in the first booth. "That puts you ahead of the game." She looked over the files in Mirelle's folder and presented her with an over-the-shoulder bag and a pad of paper. "Write down your worst fear and your deepest desire. Be literal. Take your time." The woman winked at Mirelle and wrote a large number seven on the front of the folder. She put the folder in a basket full of other folders, and waved at the next person in line.

Mirelle took a deep breath and followed the arrows on the floor. The absence of pain in her chest and legs was still a new feeling, and she suppressed a sudden urge to jog down the corridor.

At the next booth, a man in a cap pulled her folder from the basket in front of him. He inserted an envelope and handed it to her, smiling a golden toothed smile. "You will choose your future self from the envelope: your location, your situation, race, parentage. You will then find seven gifts from the available objects. These will be presented to your future self when they become necessary." He pointed to the window in the wall right next to her. Receding into the white space outside the booth for an eternity were piles upon piles of clothing, bins of toys, fruit, shoes, dishes. Tents. Sofas.

"Put them in your bag. Remember your worst fear. Your deepest desire. Those, along with the objects, are your only legacy."

"You sound like the Wizard of Oz," she said to the man. He scratched his head, but did not look offended. "Do you think I can fit a sofa inside this bag?" Mirelle asked, but the man motioned toward the window and invited the next person in line to step forward.

On a bench under the window, Mirelle sat down and put her head into her hands. She thought there'd be rest. Light and dead pets and maybe a buffet. She wasn't ready to start everything over again. Her deepest desires on earth had always involved safety or paychecks, but she knew she'd have to do better than that. How? She opened the flap of the envelope. Two cards. Easy choice. She chose the girl.

At the pile of blue sweaters, Mirelle let the boy look through her bag: An inflatable raft, a tangle of keys, and a pair of sturdy brown walking shoes. She had three more objects to choose after the sweater: three more messages sent from beyond. She pushed away the apprehension and forced herself to think instead of the way it would feel to shave her young future legs the first time. Age eleven? Twelve?

The boy looked up at her. "I'm Theo," he said.

Mirelle shook his hand and introduced herself. "Can I ask you a personal question?"

"Arrested development, I think," Theo said, not waiting for the question. "I was in a boating accident when I was eight and I got stuck with a bum body, but I grew up all right. The last time I could move freely, I was this size. That's the only explanation I can come up with. Were you this age when you died?" He swept his hand from her head to her feet.

"A bit older, I think. I was wondering."

"I don't know how all the dying part works. But my future choices are limited." He pulled his envelope out and showed her the only card inside. "There was a meltdown in my teens," he explained.

"Oh?"

"That's right. Hard to imagine that I was the one who picked that terrible life for myself."

Mirelle shrugged. "You hadn't lived it yet. How many things do you get to pass on?"

"Four gifts. You?"

"Seven."

"This sucks."

Mirelle thought it didn't suck as much as cancer, but she didn't say so. She couldn't—not to an ex-quadriplegic with suicidal tendencies. She was pain free now, but the memory of sickness wore at her like the memory of someone she used to love but didn't want to call. She'd died alone, afraid at the end, wishing for an afterlife much different than this one. Secretly, she'd always believed that people should get exactly what they want after the whole thing was over: Mormons their Celestial Kingdom, Baptists their Right Hand of God, Agnostics their Pleasant Surprises. This white room had no walls. She couldn't even sense a source of light.

They decided to go as far as they could in one direction to see if they could reach the end of the objects. Just to see what was on the other side.

"The world is big outside of America," Theo said. "And it's not like I even saw that much of America, at least not until 2000 or so, when we got the internet." They passed a woman weeping over a stack of high heel shoeboxes. "She looks famous," Theo whispered.

Mirelle couldn't place her. "Is this it? Choose a card and a few items and then go back as someone different? What's the point of a revolving door?"

Theo shook his head. "There's a point. I been here a while. You have to search for the things that will bring you the life you want. If you choose the wrong things, you can break your future self. I broke, kind of. You obviously almost broke."

"How do you know?"

"Well, seven objects is more than four, but some people have, like, fifty. And they have a whole stack of possible selves with problems like Too Many Boats. They can just about plan an entire life."

Mirelle did not believe him. "With chess boards and crock pots?"

Theo fixed her with a critical eye. He directed her to a table full of watches and demanded she pick a real Rolex from a stack of knock offs.

She had never even thought about Rolexes. "I was a public servant. I don't have a clue," she said.

"That's the difference between you and Too Many Boats," Theo replied.

Rolexes had been the least of Mirelle's worries; once she was old enough to leave the house, she was never invited back. She recalled her father wearing expensive looking cuff links and ties, but she didn't remember anything about a watch. Her parents weren't around much for fashion advice, anyway, even when she'd been properly engaged in football and high school dances.

Mirelle met Abraham in Syracuse while she was still uncomfortably inhabiting the body of a young adult male. Abraham was the first to suggest that perhaps she was not yet who she might be. They were in an acting class together first, then auditioned to be regulars in a gay political theater group called GAYTES OF JUSTICE. Abraham's roommate was brewing beer in their shared dormitory suite bathroom, so he showed up without notice one evening and installed himself in the spare bunk above Mirelle's. He brought a suitcase, stacks of CDs in cracked jewel cases, and a poster of Morrissey in his underwear.

"Shit's about to blow in that place, and I need this scholarship," he said. Not a month had passed before Mirelle convinced herself they were in love.

He was growing his usually well-kept fade into something he called a halfro, and one night after one too many Miller Lites, Mirelle let herself catch one of the longer curls between her thumb and forefinger as Abraham drifted off into a comfortably buzzed slumber.

He didn't push her away when she moved in to kiss him, but after a few minutes, he slid out from under her and went to the shared bathroom. He emerged with a small case beneath his arm and sat down on the bed across from Mirelle.

"Let me try something, Mitch?"

She leaned in to kiss him again, but he flipped open the case between them and extracted a tube of mascara. "Your eyes are amazing. I've been thinking of trying this color on you for weeks."

Mirelle looked at the tube in his hand. It was the same brand her mother used, just a shade lighter. The first of every month, Mirelle's mother visited Ingrid at the SAKS cosmetic counter to pick up her usuals. When she was allowed to accompany her mother, say if Mirelle needed a new tie for an upcoming formal or a new pair of cleats, Mirelle held her mother's purse and listened to Ingrid's suggestions for winter colors and matte finishes, night-time toner that tightened and replenished. They left with little plastic zipper bags of free samples, totes full of spongy wedges, and around the holidays, entire cases of eyeshadow with a hundred new shades to try.

They had the same skin tone, Mirelle and her mother. The same translucent eyelashes and subtle rosewood lips that began to crack the first cold front of the year.

"How did you get hold of this?" Mirelle asked.

"Wouldn't you like to know?" Abraham gently brushed Mirelle's hair back and brought her chin forward. "Look up," he said.

"You just walk in there and ask for makeup?"

"Like a supermodel," Abraham said. His breath was cool and smoky on her cheek as the mascara wetly darkened the edges of her vision. Of course, he just walked in there and asked for what he wanted. "You want to come along next time? We'll get your colors done." He opened a compact and showed Mirelle her eyes. "Look how beautiful you are," he said. .

Mirelle took the compact from him and went to the mirror over the sink. She leaned in and swallowed hard, tears springing from nowhere. Behind her, Abraham handed over the tube and assured her that the mascara was waterproof.

MIRELLE JOTTED DOWN possibilities in her notepad as she followed Theo from table to table. Maybe a trench coat. A radio headset. A book about divorce law. She felt the tiniest flicker of excitement inside her chest. She imagined her new self being born of nothing, alone in a white room; at thirteen, in the dining room of another strange family, praying before a meal; at thirty- two, living around the corner from a handsome, clever man who claimed to love Miles Davis but only knew his music from a college music appreciation class. Above all, the clothes against her skin, the men turning their heads to watch her pass. The home within her self, finally. At least she would be a girl. That part wouldn't be a struggle next time around.

Another life. More bad food, head colds, roaches, awkward sex. Dogs, hot rain, global crises. Coffee. She let her fingertips graze the tops of several ferns, and spotted a familiar-looking lamp in the hands of a large woman two tables over. She grabbed Theo's hand and walked over.

"What?" The woman drew the lamp to her chest protectively as they approached.

"That lamp just looks familiar. I'll give it back. I don't want to keep it." The woman handed the lamp over, and sure enough, on the bottom of the base was a crack in the shape of Florida.

"This was ours!" She turned to show Theo, who seemed only mildly interested. "It was in my mother's sitting room. I tried to break it one day because she refused to take me to a party." Mirelle found she didn't want to give it up when the woman smiled politely and reached again for the lamp.

Theo watched her take the lamp from Mirelle. "Tasha?" he asked.

Tasha tucked the lamp into her bag and raised her eyebrows at Theo. "What are you still doing here, Theo?"

"I told you I'd been here a long time," he said to Mirelle. "But I haven't been here as long as Tasha."

"So what?" said Tasha, throwing her head back defensively.

"So nothing. I just thought you'd get a handle on things by now."

Tasha's face closed into itself. "I can't," she said. She dug through her bag and retrieved a worn looking envelope. "One card. One. I can't go back on this card."

Mirelle took the envelope from her. *Afghanistan, educated woman, mother of three girls.*

"I know what it's like. I was a Marine." Tasha straightened a little at the mention of her work on earth. Mirelle could see the remnants of a military stance beneath what was likely Tasha's burial dress, but her eyes were soft and dewey and not at all like the eyes of her clients who had come home from the desert. She looked reachable.

"How long were you there?" Mirelle asked.

"Two tours. Too many."

"You'll be on the other side now, though," Theo said. Mirelle could tell that this was not a comforting statement for Tasha. "So, what, you're just going to wander around here for eternity?"

"I haven't decided. I think I might."

"Is that allowed?" Mirelle asked.

"I don't know who's in charge, actually." Tasha sighed and looked around. "Nobody's stopped me so far."

"Well, carrying that lamp around is not going to help you make a decision about going back," Theo said.

"So what? I like it." Tasha snatched the card back from Mirelle and turned away abruptly.

"I can't believe it," Mirelle said as she watched Tasha stalk off between the tables.

"*That* was confusing," Theo asked, clearly exasperated. "Why in god's name would you have passed that useless lamp on to yourself?"

"I don't know. I didn't exactly use it to kill an intruder and save my family. It was just there. My mother loved it." Mirelle shrugged. "I wonder how many people are just killing time like Tasha."

"I wish I had a card to give her," Theo said.

"You can't just trade lives with someone else."

"Who says?"

"It just doesn't seem right."

She couldn't decide a thing about her deepest desire or her worst fear, and felt at a disadvantage because most of it seemed as distant as a dream from three nights previous. She asked Theo if he felt the same way.

"I know what I know," he said, shoving a pair of sunglasses deep into his bag.

MIRELLE STOPPED SLEEPING after her first makeover. She lay awake listening to Abraham breathe instead, wondering how she had neglected to notice such a crucial element of basic selfhood. For a while, gender panic eclipsed the plain fact that Abraham didn't return her love. She leapt back and forth through her own history, piecing together clues that had seemed to merely point in the direction of effeminate—never actually feminine.

By way of contribution, Abraham kept the fridge and the printer stocked. During the week, he tossed off translations for French and Spanish classes while working his way through one cheap beer after another. Mirelle struggled to keep her eyes open in class and rarely finished her assignments with any alacrity. Instead of working alongside him in the evenings, she watched Abraham study and thought about what it might feel like to wear a bra.

On the weekends, he coaxed Mirelle out of the dorm for rehearsals, though she refused to audition for parts and insisted on writing or working backstage.

"But it's *acceptable* to wear makeup on stage," he teased one day on the way home from rehearsal.

"I prefer to watch my words in action," she said, unconvincingly.

"You lie," he said. "You just don't want a boy part." It was maddening the way he threw those words around when she could barely utter the truth. He had no idea.

She loved him every time he slept with a professor, unsuccessfully wooed a basketball player, or shopped through her clothes to prepare for a night of sneaking past bouncers. Sometimes she went with him, but it felt like death each time he trained his beautiful brown eyes on someone else.

THEO SAID HE needed to rest, so they picked a bench beside a fountain and sat down. He opened his bag and began unloading its contents. Mirelle watched the passersby. Most of them walked alone, looking bewildered. She elbowed Theo and he looked up to watch the weeping celebrity pass, pushing a wheelbarrow.

"What do you think her deepest desire is?" Mirelle asked.

"No idea. But I'll tell you mine," he said. He held up a tennis ball and a pair of green socks. "After you advise me on which is most ridiculous. Ball? Socks?"

Mirelle held out her hands and Theo relinquished the items. He flipped through the pages in his notepad. "My deepest desire is to be alone in my thoughts and my actions," he read. "It took me forever to get that much down, and it's terrible. Tasha tried to help me make it better, but she has no idea what she's doing, either."

Mirelle stood up and threw the ball as far as she could and watched it disappear. "There are no walls?"

"Focus," Theo said.

Mirelle sat down and looked at Theo. "I think we are supposed to somehow prepare our future selves to achieve that deepest desire, Theo, and I think you might be wrong about how it's all done."

"I should keep the socks, then?"

"No. You probably don't need anything."

"That's not what the guy with the gold teeth said."

"You made it through a shit-hole life, Theo. You didn't hurt yourself or anyone else—"

"Not that I didn't try—"

"—and you're about to embark on another life, just as difficult. Quite possibly. A tennis ball and a pair of socks won't make or break you."

"It looks like maybe you want the socks for yourself."

"Shut up, Theo. I mean, I think *I* can do this next life. In fact, after all this meaningless wandering, I'm kind of looking forward to going back. It won't be easy, but there are drugs that can adjust my brain chemistry, and I know I figured out how to make family out of friends last time around." Mirelle thought of Abraham, in another lifetime, teaching her to walk in heels.

"Maybe fewer cards, fewer objects, means you're ready to move on after this next life."

"On to what?"

"I can't say. But this can't be *it*."

"I think you're deluded."

Mirelle shrugged. "Maybe I am. And maybe you're too comfortable here." Theo shot her a look that did not belong to a child. "You want to hang out with Tasha the rest of your days? Never grow up? It's nice to be tall, Theo," she said. "We'll go together."

"You don't have to take care of me, Mirelle," Theo said.

THE MEMORY OF the gun glistened in a sharp wet night, years and years after they'd moved out of the dorm and into a faux Victorian with vaulted ceilings and bedrooms connected by a long bathroom. There was a big autumn moon, reflected in the puddles on the sidewalks, everywhere at once. The air outside Club DeVine was a welcome surprise – a rainstorm had ushered in a cold front while they'd been inside, and the sweat beneath Mirelle's clothes turned chill the minute the doors closed behind them. She'd been dancing most of the night with a beautiful young dyke who had a bar code tattooed at the base of her neck. Since hrt, she'd found her tastes ventured from beautiful fey men to beautiful butch women—something about the hard line of the shoulders and the softness at the top of the thigh.

She and Abraham lived together like there could never be another way. He'd been dating Justin for almost two years, long distance. She'd gone back to graduate school after losing her job for wearing a dress into the office, put her near-brain-dead mother into assisted living, and fallen out of love with Abraham three times.

Abraham stuffed his feathered vest into her bag and reached for her hand on the street. They did this as much for protection as for closeness. From the back, they could pass as a straight couple headed home after drinks.

"So sad we're going home alone," he said, with mock sincerity.

"Speak for yourself. I got some digits in my purse."

"Please, Mirelle, Barcode Butch is still in diapers. Do not call her unless you want to converse solely about drag king performance art and socialized medicine."

Mirelle squeezed Abraham's hand. "Call Justin when we get home and I'll confirm your victory over temptation tonight. I saw that glitter boy all up in your face. I could read his mind."

"It's seven in the morning there."

"So what?"

Abraham leaned in affectionately. His head upon her shoulder was the last thing Mirelle felt before she came to with metal in her mouth and a knee in her crotch.

"I WONDER WHAT would happen if I chose more than my allotted items," Theo said. She threw the socks into the fountain, feeling guilt-free for littering. They sponged a little before sinking beneath the surface of the water.

"Want to hear my biggest fear?"

"Not right now," said Mirelle.

They couldn't agree on which direction to go. People were using it like a roundabout, stopping to rest at the base and then taking off in a different direction. There was only white above, white below, white ahead, white behind.

It was difficult not to bite down on the barrel of the gun that had torn the inside of her cheek so deeply she was choking on blood. His knee ground bright white pain into her thighs and stomach, and she thought she might pass straight out into the static shrinking her vision. He was saying things to her, things she couldn't hear, or things she didn't understand. Mirelle raised an arm. He swung at it with his free hand, and someone else's boot came down hard on her palm.

Then he was up. The gun was gone. She coughed, turned her head and vomited blood. There were three or four of them, the moon like a spotlight over their heads.

"You want me to take care of your little problem?" He was saying. Or one of them was saying. She heard someone mutter, almost kindly, "Get up, freak."

She tried to stand, but dropped her head into her hands when the new pain and sight of blood on her skirt threatened to knock her out again. Two of the guys stepped forward, lifted her to her feet, and pushed her against the wall. The gun that was once in her mouth was now pointed directly at the bloodstain between her legs.

"You want me to take care of you? Say the word and I make your dreams come true. It's what you want? Right?"

Mirelle didn't answer. One of her back molars was loose.

In a singsong voice, he continued: "Or you can say no, no sir, I love my dick. God made me a man, and men *love* their dicks. Just that, and I'll walk away."

One of the men holding her up let go to light a cigarette. He exhaled into her face and said, "I'm bored, man. It's late. Just do it or whatever."

Mirelle spat. The left side of her peripheral vision was gone. "Don't shoot," she said, quietly.

"Not good enough," said the one with the gun. The guy smoking a cigarette sighed loudly.

"Where's Abraham?" Mirelle asked.

He rushed her, his face in her face, the metal now pushed against her pelvic bone. "We already killed the faggot," he said. "Speaking of dick lovers."

Mirelle found his eyes. She told him she loved her dick.

"Do you ever get hungry here?" Mirelle asked Theo. He shook his head. They approached a table of firearms. "Know anything about handguns?"

"Not much, but not for lack of trying." Theo hefted a semi-automatic rifle off the table.

"This might be the cure they're talking about," she said. "For the mental illness."

"*That's* not morbid." He put his eye to the sight, aiming at nothing. "You're not supposed to kill anyone."

Mirelle dropped a 9 millimeter into her bag. Perfect size for a purse, for a small hand. Two items to go.

Theo replaced the AR-15 with a .22 instead. "For food. In case, I'm dropped back in the middle of the apocalypse. You think of that?"

Abraham wasn't dead. He was unconscious, but not shot. Mirelle crawled to him and lowered her swollen face to his chest to make sure she could hear his heartbeat. Then dragged herself into a twenty-four hour gas station to call an ambulance. She returned to Abraham and waited for half an hour, her fingers near his mouth, counting every breath.

They let her ride with him to the ER, where she had difficulty explaining the situation with any clarity. The nurse called her Mitchell and sewed her back together without ever making eye contact. They threw away her skirt and found her a pair of sweat pants.

She called Abraham's parents in Puerto Rico and soothed his mother the best she could in broken Spanish.

"I laughed in that fuckwad's face," Abraham told Mirelle. A day later, his left eye still swollen shut, teary pus caught in his long black lashes. "That's why he jacked me up. I was never scared, and he knew it."

"Hell of a way to prove your manhood," she said, unfolding an ice compress from his crusted, yellowing forehead.

"Yeah? Well, where were you, Mirelle?"

"What do you want me to say? I was enjoying a cold beverage while they beat the fuck out of you? I was unconscious, Abe."

"You also never fight for shit."

Mirelle turned her back. She returned to the kitchen to refill his water bottle, thinking he couldn't mean what he said. Only upset that he hadn't had the chance to protect himself. Mirelle heard Abraham on the phone that night, speaking in low tones long after he'd said good night to her.

Mirelle went back to work. Her mouth healed slowly. She removed her own stitches instead of returning to the hospital. At night, she watched TV next to Abraham on the couch. They didn't talk much.

It took Justin a few days to pack Abraham's things, and another few days to get the doctor's clearance for Abraham to ride across country. His face hadn't even lost its patchwork bruising, and Abraham was gone.

"I FEAR THERE'S no end to this place," Mirelle said, looking around. Theo asked to see her bag again. She handed it to him as she circled a pile of things with little screens that lit up when touched. She had no idea what they might be used for, but she chose one and began to experiment. A man next to her spoke quietly into the screen, listening to something that she couldn't hear. She looked up to ask Theo his opinion, and didn't see him. She called his name a couple of times, returning to the spot where she'd left him. His bag was there, emptied of all objects, save his original blue sweater. She dug around and below the sweater she found that he'd left her own notepad and her own envelope, minus the one card she'd chosen for her future self.

She ran a few futile steps toward nothing and then sank onto a bench. Her future as a woman was gone, gone with Theo. Anger punched its way through the fog of distance that had overtaken her memories. Biggest fear: being blindsided. Complete loss of control.

She opened the envelope and pulled out the remaining card. *Male, Ritual Abuse at Hands of Trusted Family Friend, Divorced Parents, Southern United States.*

Mirelle retrieved her notebook, dropped the bag on the floor and kicked it underneath a chair. Beneath her worst fear, she wrote her greatest desire: Retribution. Then she set out for the beginning again.

Radical Reorganization

Genevieve

EDDIE HAS A hot cup of coffee in his hands even though it's 107 degrees on the patio of the coffee shop. There's a plate of bagels between us, cream cheese melting. Eddie claims he's not hungry, but I'm sure he will finish the plate before we leave. It's only a few days before gestation, so we've decided to spend as much of the advance as we can on rich food and coffee.

"I've already been through the preliminaries," I tell him. "And I'm pretty sure there's someone kind of following me around, making sure I don't take off."

Eddie raises his eyebrows like he doesn't believe me, so I point at the dusty blue car at the curb beside the coffee shop. Waves of heat emanate from the hood. "See that car?"

Eddie turns around and waves at the man in the car. "What does it matter? You're not going anywhere, right?"

"I guess not."

"We'll find each other," he says, splitting the bagel into quarters. "After this is all over." His tone is light, but I can tell he's worried. The man in the blue car has worried him. There's no wind and the sky is free of clouds. We're under one of those useless slatted wooden patio roofs that keep off neither rain nor sun. Though I'm not hot yet, I adjust the temperature levels at my wrist.

"I just wish you'd told me earlier," he says with his mouth full. I don't point out that the one time I tried to talk to him about my decision, he thought I was going on about suicide too much and threatened to call the hospital.

"I didn't want to fight about it," I say.

On the way home, I stop by the Brown Hall and buy a nice camera/screen and tripod. It's something I've always wanted, something my father vaguely promised me for my twentieth birthday and never delivered. I've never taken pictures before, but it's very cool to think of something expensive and then just walk into a store and buy it.

Back at the apartment, I spend the evening setting up the three point softbox, umbrella, and screen. The equipment takes up most of the room in my efficiency, but I like the way it looks—purposeful—and I enjoy stepping around everything to get from one corner of the apartment to the other. The pocked walls and water-warped floors suddenly take on an artistic purity instead of the sad, neglected stain of the day I moved in. Maybe it's the new lighting, or the smell of ripped cardboard and stainless steel. I open a bottle of white wine and disrobe and start taking pictures of my body from all angles, in all positions. I tell myself that I may need records for the future, in case I forget and get ungrateful.

As it turns out, I'm not half bad with the camera. The next day, I check out a couple of instructional videos and then leave the apartment to try my eye on the world outside.

The sidewalk is white hot; I can feel the soles of my shoes get a little sticky when I spend too long in one place, so I move to the turf and make my way down the block to the park. There are children running around in old coolersuits—the kind with tubes, but all the adults are gathered together under the shade in various states of undress. There's a pool nearby, but nobody is in the water. In this part of town, it's not smart to trust the water. I take a few pictures of the kids on the slides, but their fun seems forced so I walk over to the gaggle of parents under the dome. I have my camera/screen out in front of my face, and one of the parents asks to see it, reaching out to take it from me. I snap the picture before he can get to me, and I already know that it'll be a good shot. The look on his face is elated and greedy. When I lower the camera/screen so he can see my face, he withdraws his hand in horror and I snap that picture too.

I always thought those people who talked about how photographers were "capturing moments of a story" were full of shit, but I kind of see where they're coming from now. It's not the story of the outside world—it's my story. This is the before. In a couple of months, there will be an after.

In September, Dr. Akachi knocked on my door as I was getting dressed to walk to Eddie's for dinner. I was already late because I'd discovered yet another tiny hole in my coolersuit, and I'd been looking for the patch kit, growing hungrier by the minute.

"Good afternoon, Genevieve?" He sounded Nigerian, just a hint of musicality in his accent.

"No interviews," I said, closing the door.

"I'm not a journalist," he said from the other side. "I'm a geneticist. I came to speak with you about my work."

I opened the door a crack. "Show me your ID," I said. "And it better say something about genetics on it."

Dr. Akachi fumbled around in his pockets, muttering *of course, of course* until he could flash a Fallingwater Institute id/screen at me. He was maybe 60, with hair beginning to gray at his temples. He had on one of those new transparent coolersuits that everyone was clamoring for. Beneath it, he was sporting a lovely gray sweater vest and dark blue jeans.

"I won't take up much of your time, Genevieve," he said, pocketing his ID and spreading his hands as though he'd just performed a magic trick. "But I am working on something that may interest you. Maybe you know my name from the documentary? Dr. Bronte Akachi?"

"I'm not passing these genes on, if you're here for eggs or something." I did not mention the stipulation of my probation that ordered immediate termination of any pregnancy, accidental or otherwise. "If you'll excuse me, I'm on my way to a job interview." It was a lie, but I hadn't eaten all day and it was Eddie's turn to cook.

"I can offer money," he said quickly. "Money even for the next hour? Just to listen."

I pulled the chain back and let him in. I saw him register the two laptops in pieces on my desk as he reached into his pocket. He offered me a hundred dollars and smiled when I took it.

"You are looking for a job?" He asked.

"Who isn't?" Jobs were difficult to find, I'd been told, even if you didn't have a tracking device stuck to the side of your head. I'd had some freelance luck with data entry, but once my laptop crashed and I missed a deadline, that was that.

"Times are hard," he agreed, but I could tell he was only repeating what he'd heard on the news. Times were not hard for people like him. The lines that ringed the eyes of the rest of us were missing from his face, and his shoes were new. Dr. Akachi took a deep breath and looked like he could use a drink. I thought of offering him some water, but my supply was lower than I liked.

He sat down on the coach. "What is your life like? Are you happy?"

"That's not really any of your business," I said. The past few years, journalists had been sneaky, some of them so kind that my feelings were hurt when I discovered what they were after.

"Of course not, but if you had a chance to start over completely, do you think you would take the opportunity?"

"Like witness protection? I'm hardly a victim."

"No, not like witness protection." He pulled a flexible screen from his bag and it began to glow at his touch. I'd never seen one of these new ones in person.

I sat down beside him, sliding the hundred-dollar bill between my palms and wondering if he'd offer more if I kept him there for longer than an hour.

"Look here," he said, as an image lit up the screen. I leaned in to see it, and caught Dr. Akachi's sharp, verdant aftershave. On the screen was a realistically rendered translucent, pea-pod shaped vessel, situated in a tank of some sort. He glanced at me, eyes alight.

In response to my silence, Dr. Akachi said "Allow me to speak frankly. You are a prisoner of your own making right now. My benefactor and I are well aware of your situation. We don't harbor any ill will toward you, but we *would* like to partner with you. We have the technology to recreate you, to re-scramble your parents' DNA and see what comes out. Not just that. Using the metamorphosis process of a butterfly as our template, we can, if you pardon the expression, boil you down to the basics again, and then grow you into any age you like." He touched the screen and a computer-generated body appeared in the pod. "Radical Reorganization. In this case, we'd want to set you back to 17. To study your physical and psychological make-up in the years that led up to the murder of your parents." I watched the body begin to change shape, and then disappear completely. In another three seconds, another body appeared in its place.

Dr. Akachi took a deep breath and touched the screen again. "Be assured that you are under no obligation to accept our offer. We only wanted to gauge your interest first. Allow me a little bit more of your time."

A house appeared on the screen. It sat on a wooded street, tucked deep into some suburb. A part of me I thought long buried began to ache. "The tracking device *we* have for you is hidden away inside your body. No more temple tracker. You will be free to go and come as you please. Plenty of money, nice house. You can go to school, find a job, be an artist. No one will know you. Studies suggest that you will have some memory of your previous life, but that is no matter. We only wish to study who you are and who you become in those years between 17 and 20. After you are 20, we check in less regularly. But your salary continues for the rest of your life."

He pointed to the house on the screen. "This is where you live. Inside the garage is a scooter. All yours. The refrigerator is stocked at all times." He looked at the coolersuit patch kit on the coffee table. "Plus newer coolersuits; the very best."

"You think about this, Genevieve," he said kindly, handing me a card. "If you wish to know more, you may find me here. You will have questions, I'm sure." His mouth set itself much the way my mother's would when she was about to let me in on what she called *the truth of the situation*.

"Understand that this is not something you should discuss with anyone. If you should choose to tell anyone about this, my—our—benefactor will not like it. We have no wish to harm you, but are prepared to take measures if we are challenged. I will not contact you again, and will begin looking for another subject at the end of this month."

I watched him pack his screen away and sling his bag over one shoulder. I liked his eyes. He let himself out, turning to thank me before opening the door. "I hope we meet again."

After he left, I put the card on the table and drank some water, hoping I could stave off dizziness until I got some food. I finished patching the hole in my coolersuit and started the long trek to Eddie's. It was dark now, and I knew he'd be mad. He might even have already eaten everything, but I had no way of getting ahold of him to tell him I was just running late. On the walk over, I passed the Green Hall. There was this memory on repeat in my head that evening; the one in which my mother and father were bickering in a broken-down manner in the front seat while I watched a DVD on a little portable player in my lap. I had earphones on, but could still hear the hiss of their voices when they'd quiet into real cruelty. My mother, especially, rarely said aloud the worst of her thoughts, which she called the *truth of the situation*. I looked up, just as we were passing the Green Hall, to see people dancing in the street outside the building. I pulled my earphones off in time to hear both the chest-thrumming beat of Conjunto music and the end of my mother's whispered sentence: "*she's never going to be normal and you know it.*" The dancing people were holding signs and jumping up and down to the music. One woman was standing on the shoulders of a man, her fists in the air and her mouth open in a scream or a song.

I asked who would never be normal, and my mother looked back at me, smiling quickly and kindly. "Oh, just somebody at work," she said, reaching back to pat my knee with an elegant hand. Then she looked at my father with bright eyes and asked him where he had made us reservations for dinner.

For years, I remembered the dancing people, and for years I believed it was the woman at work who'd never be normal. But the memory never lost its focus, and every time I spotted the Green Hall, I'd play it over again. The people, the dancing, the hissing, the beat that came through the street, shaking the frame of our car, pulsing up my spine and stopping at the place where my throat hit the bottom of my chin.

Eddie wasn't mad, but he had eaten the food. It was so late that he'd already changed into his pajamas.

"Damnit, Eddie, I am so hungry today," I told him, as I collapsed onto the stool at the counter in his kitchen. He held his hands up like what did you want me to do?

His dark hair had grown out and he was starting to resemble Jesus in a bathrobe again. I would have eaten the food and we both knew it. I thought about the hundred in my pocket. I knew if I broke it, I'd just keep spending and keep spending until it was gone, rent be damned. But the hundred wasn't even close to what I owed for rent, so what did it matter?

"I bet you're still hungry," I said, pulling the hundred out of my pocket.

"Where did you get that?"

"I earned it," I said.

"Another interview?"

"Yeah. Let me spend the evening on your work/screen and I'll pay for as much takeout as you want," I said. He would have let me anyway. Since mine had broken, I'd spent about every evening at his house job-searching, but I wanted to make it seem like we were trading services. Like our friendship had ever been close to reciprocal.

The next morning, I woke up hot and angry. A huge green field grasshopper had found its way into my kitchenette sometime in the night and availed itself of the acoustics. I made one attempt to quiet it—I could see its long febrile body vibrating on top of my counter—by throwing a shoe in its general direction.

I'm afraid of bugs. Of their vacant consciousness and unshakable wills to exist in hidden spaces. It sang or chirped or whatever all night long and I felt trapped. The heat was next to unbearable, and I was scared to wear my coolersuit to bed for fear I'd tear it open again.

When the sun finally rose, I went outside, lit a cigarette on the landing, and thought about Dr. Akachi's offer.

THE NIGHT I killed my parents was icy—up until then, my favorite kind of weather. I was home for the winter break, and the streets were flinty with cold. My parents worked through the holidays and often only took off for a few days after New Year's Eve, when the world began to come to its senses. My mother never liked to waste her days off when other people were clogging the city. She bought her gifts, sensibly, all year long, and was never caught out in the crush of shoppers who had to face needlessly high prices on Christmas Eve. Her presents were always wrapped by the end of November. I knew they'd be thoughtful. She took silent notes on things my father and I mentioned only in passing. I never saw her more satisfied as when we opened presents we'd forgotten we'd asked for. I wanted a camera/screen that year; they'd just come out and were so expensive and showy that I thought my Dad just might go for it. I was not afraid of crowds, and even loved the feeling of being present and alone in the throngs of humanity. I spent the weeks before Christmas walking miles of malls, looking at all the camera sales and waiting in hot chocolate lines with Eddie. That particular evening we ended up on the floor of the bookstore up north of town, reading comics and magazines we were never going to buy.

When I got home from the bookstore that afternoon, the house was dark and cold. I let myself in and flipped the hall light on. There was a growling, a spitting sound in the front room, like a nature documentary turned up too loud. I put down my bag and walked to the end of the front hall to find my father gesturing wildly in the darkness, the phone pinned between his right ear and shoulder, a lit cigarette in his left hand. I caught his shadowy profile as he lifted the cigarette, and where his face should have been was instead a vast empty chasm.

I ARRIVE AT the institute about an hour early, but the nurse greets me and kindly offers to give me a tour of the place I'll be gestating. The Pod matches the pictures Dr. Akachi showed me during the transfusions, but it's much bigger than I thought it would be. It's empty, and the translucent, protein-infused skin on the outside is warm to the touch.

"There's enough room in there for three of me."

"We had to accommodate for all possibilities," said the nurse. "There were a couple of cases of gigantism on your Dad's side way back." I imagine myself reorganized into a giant woman with hands the size of dinner plates.

"Most people with gigantism don't live past their 30s," she adds, with a hint of sympathy. Just a hint, though, because she knows I know what I've chosen. She points to a plastic tube attached to the Pod. "There's your entrance," she says. "It's sterile."

The nurse leads me through an airlock and into a tiled room with numbered showerheads along the back wall. She sits me down on a stool and shaves my head with a vacuum attachment that sucks the hair away as it is cut.

Then she shows me a tube of a white substance. "To prevent any pain," she explains, as she slathers it over the newly exposed skin of my scalp. At the first shower, she hands me a washcloth and tells me I will be scrubbing each body part for thirty seconds.

"I'll time you. We'll start with your face."

By the end of it, the nerves beneath my skin are singing. When I finish, the nurse asks me to move to the second shower and I repeat the process under a stream of metallic-smelling water. There must be a painkiller in this stream, however, because my nerves calm down immediately and I am able to scrub my belly like a platter in a sink. The next three showers are rinses, and the nurse directs me toward another airlock that leads to one more shower that leaves me feeling oily and light. Nurse 2, dressed in a white space suit, leads me out into the sterile walkway. As I walk toward the Pod, I have a thought that I am thinking the very last thoughts I will think as this person. I have a thought that my body does not really house the bomb. I have a thought that maybe I will die. Relief courses through my veins as I push my right hand through the Pod's membrane and enter the future.

MY FATHER GREW up beautiful and emerged from a quietly treacherous childhood with a low-grade lust for cruelty. He fell in love with my mother, who had by her early twenties developed a reflective carapace and a studied stately beauty, and they moved to the outskirts of Austin in the mid-2000s to start a family. She loved him back, I think, in the way a snake loves a mongoose.

Our house was a three story modern with windows that let light into places light wasn't ordinarily welcomed. In my room, there was a long strip of red and blue stained glass that ran ankle-height along the outside wall. When I was small, I once asked my mother to sew tiny curtains for the windows so that no birds could fly by and see inside my room.

For years, this was the primary tale my mother told about my childhood, can you believe this, birds flying by and looking at her! Curtains?

My father had once thought the fireplace to be superfluous, but as I grew up and the temperatures became more and more extreme, the fireplace became one of his favorite features of the house. The open-floor metal and glass design of the first level of the house made it feel a little like we were living onset in a 1970s sci-fi film, despite the floor to ceiling windows across the back. Our fireplace was its own sleek island, with a titanium grille that hung like a curtain in front of the flames. I loved that you could see the fire's light and movement from practically anywhere on the first floor.

I grew up in that house, all steel and glass, unsure of what we were supposed to be doing with all that space. I learned from my father that more children were supposed to follow me, but that something had gone wrong during my mother's pregnancy, something so difficult and frightening, that she had never conceded to go off the pill again. I hung out with Briana most days after school in her house that was just as big as ours, but echoing with the voices of about ten or twelve kids and aunts and grandparents who lived in all those rooms. At dusk, when her house began smelling of onions or curry or brisket, I was sent home to my own kitchen to await whichever parent returned with food.

Nobody cooked, but food was important to all of us. From a young age, I was very clear about how much food should be ingested by a normal human body of my age. One morning, my mother surprised me in the kitchen.

"Time to learn to pack your own lunch," she told me, gesturing to the island before her. There were doughnuts, chocolate and powdered, carrot sticks, a pouch of tuna. Cheese crackers in little 100 calorie packs, and a few of those breakfast biscuits that were basically just cookies. A jar of peanut butter. Some pita bread under a pile of bananas, and about five different types of granola bars.

"This will be fun!" she said, handing me a paper bag. "Choose anything you like and stop at 800 calories. That's a good lunch, don't you think?"

"Is that what I've been having?" I asked.

My mother sniffed coldly. "I don't know what your father's been doing, dear."

I watched her face while I reached for my first item—carrots. I knew the doughnuts were out because I'd heard her reprimand my father for buying them. She looked pleased and asked me to read the calorie count and serving size on the package.

"It's never too early," she said, entering the count into her phone while I dropped the carrots into my lunch bag. "What's next?" she asked brightly, as though she were a fun mom, and this was a normal thing to do. I made the same lunch every day for the next five years: carrot sticks, one granola bar, peanut butter spread between two slices of pita bread, and a banana. Every once in a while, she'd slip a note into the bag, with an extra 200 calories of nuts, as a treat.

IN THE YEARS following their deaths, I willingly submitted myself to a battery of psychological tests, neurological assessments, and personality analyses. That I was as confused as they were about the murders was fascinating to them, and pretty soon my name had inspired entire journals full of articles speculating about my sexuality, behavior, desires, regrets, and relationships. The media went full-court press with my story, running it all over every news outlet and publishing thinly veiled fictional accounts of my crimes: *Austin Twirler Murders Parents With Bare Hands*. My high school friends were paid exorbitant sums of money to give up pictures and letters and personal stories. Briana was the worst. She wrote an entire book about our friendship with a ghost writer and claimed that she'd been my first girlfriend. This wasn't true. I'd never had a girlfriend and probably never would.

I am sure it was because of this media intervention that I didn't see any jail time. Instead, I got a temple tracker and probation for the rest of my life. I believed that the tracking device was better than being locked up. My device was hacked within hours, however, and there were 24-hour real-time feeds that gave my whereabouts to anyone who cared to know. The police showed little concern; given the seriousness of my previous crimes, more than one of them insinuated that I should be able to protect myself just fine.

I changed my last name to something more ordinary and considered plastic surgery for a few years after the acquittal, but the temple tracker stuck to the side of my head could never be hidden. As a recognizable monster loose on the street, there were a few times I wished for a prison sentence just so I could escape the spectacle. Just a few times, though. The truth is that plastic surgery, changing my name, moving neighborhoods—all that was superficial. It might have made my life outside easier, but it could never have silenced the tick of the time bomb that was my heart.

Nobody believed me, in those months following the deaths of my parents, that they were no better or worse than anyone else's. My father's everyday manner was vaguely threatening, shoulders a little too high, gait a little too stiff, but he was often thoughtful and compassionate if he saw me in distress. I thought him handsome, though his hair was thin and his breath often smelled like a full ashtray left in the rain.

Long after I'd grown too big for it, he'd pull me onto the couch next to him while he worked, put a heavy arm over my shoulders, and hold me tight until I yelped for release. Once I'd squirmed free, he'd play-scold me for interrupting his work with such a foolish ploy for his affections. It was one of those things I missed when he was gone. He belonged to a group of model airplane enthusiasts, and some nights he came home smelling strongly of model glue, a little high from the contact. Those nights he was talkative and excitable, and might even try to explain something new he'd tried in the workshop.

When my parents happened to be in the same room, they'd resume their tired, never-ending fight about nothing and everything, and I'd do my best to disappear out the nearest door before they tried to include me. A wrong answer from me could alienate one or the other for an indeterminate number of days, or elicit a quick, sound slap from my mother.

I loved my parents, in fact, and missed them once they were gone. In all my years at home, I'd never suspected my family to be any different than most. Half of my graduating class was proudly bulimic; we'd been raised by *The Biggest Loser* and mothers who believed that carbs were one of the sweet temptations that we conquer as Christian soldiers, along with internet porn and weed.

Eddie's dad was a well-known high school art teacher with wandering hands, and Briana's mom never left the house because she was convinced it was the devil in the sewers beneath the roads who caused car accidents. The fact that my parents were never in the same room at the same time struck none of my friends as odd. They were accustomed to households with violent, wall-shaking fights and secrets no one could forget. My house was at least quiet, if not exactly peaceful. I had an entire second floor to myself where I slept and listened to music and had pizzas delivered at all hours of the night. My silent mother and defensive father were the least of our worries.

Eddie once confessed that while he was being questioned, he had this wild urge to make up horrible things that my mother and father had done to all of us. For my protection, he said. For his own protection, he went straight from high school graduation to an EMTS Academy, claiming he never again wanted to show up to a tragedy unprepared.

It's a little too warm inside the pod. Dr. Akachi appears at my feet and gives me a thumbs-up while I try hard not to care about my naked body. I don't have to care about it anymore because I'm about to shed it. I tell myself he's looking at a corpse. I hear him announce to the other white coats in the room that the oxygenated amniotic fluid will feel like a hot bath, and then he leans into a microphone and asks me if I can hear him.

"Inside and out," I say.

"While you're in the fluid, raise your hand over your head for yes or point at your foot for no," he says. I raise my right hand over my head. His voice is as rich and warm as the fluid slowly rising over my ankles. He reminds me that I will be able to breathe in the solution and to calm my heart if I can. He's got my vitals on a screen in front of him, and a camera is filming every moment of the next two months. As the fluid hits my chest, I duck my head under just like I used to at the lake when it was cold. He's right. The fluid is only a little thicker than water, but I'm floating effortlessly. I can breathe just fine, only without taking any air into my lungs. I feel infused with light and wind; I don't miss gravity. I can see just fine, too. I twist around to find Dr. Akachi, who has climbed the stairs to the pod and now stands with his hands on the membrane. His face is wide open with wonder and satisfaction and I give him a big smile and return his thumbs-up.

MY MOTHER HAD a lovely group of friends who came by on Friday evenings for poker. They were Mrs. Hanratty, Mrs. Fulton, Mrs. Brighton, and Mrs. Solis. It started out as a jigsaw puzzle group, but soon got too competitive. My mother thought the addition of cocktails, dice and a five-dollar ante might be a better fit for them all, so she stocked up on Jack Daniels every Friday after work and enforced a no-heels rule at the door.

"Have you seen Dad since you've been home?" I asked my mother as I pulled the pizza menu off the fridge. *Because I'm worried that he has no face.* Eddie and Briana were headed over at nine. Slate light filtered through the windows; beyond the bare trees, I could see a close white sky and I wondered if we might see snow.

"He's not home for hours yet," she told me, stepping up onto the kickstool so she could reach the stemless wineglasses. "But don't bother him tonight. He's got a lot on his plate lately."

"I just saw him in the front room," I said. *With no face.*

My mother turned to look at me, then raised her head to think.

"No you didn't," she said, finally. "Rinse these, will you?" She handed me a couple of glasses from her perch.

I said nothing as I turned on the hot water tap. She stepped off the stool with a wine glass over each finger. Over the sound of the water, I heard that sharp hissing again. I tried once more: "He was on the phone, and maybe he was wearing a mask of some sort?"

I think I'm probably taller now than she was then, but on that day I looked up into her eyes and felt small. She had a righteous nose; if you got past that you were usually in enemy territory. She looked at me but didn't say anything. Then she made a shooing motion with the cup towel and told me that she knew it was the third pizza this week and that I wouldn't have good metabolism forever.

"Your dad is fine," she said, toward the front hallway. "Just leave him alone tonight."

ONCE THE FLUID has covered my head, Dr. Akachi tells me he will be tightening the membrane a little bit at a time. He asks me if I can hear him, and I raise my hand above my head, even though I'm upside down.

"You won't feel claustrophobic, Dearest," he says. "You'll be unconscious by the time it gets tight."

I don't feel the pull of gravity like I do on the outside, and my limbs already feel as though there's nothing but water holding the joints in place. Can they be dissolving already? I close my eyes and when I open them again Dr. Akachi is gone. There is only the lens of the camera to wave to.

Richard

I wake up long before I can open my eyes, though this is impossible to explain to anyone. Before I can speak or sit up, I hear the words of the people who are monitoring my progress: their detached worries over a fever that won't leave a child, a paycheck that has been stolen by the sudden appearance of basement mold, the final straw on a television show that will never be watched again. I feel very sure they are not human. As I listen, I try to figure out why they've been programmed to sound concerned while their faces click and whir behind masks. It's the opposite of comforting.

It's almost as if I can see, almost as though I'm sitting there with them in the room. Which of course, I am. But no one is treating me as though I am present. It's just a regular hospital room, the best I can make out, and there is only one source of light above me. I can't move, but I don't feel upset about it. In fact, the low humming of the machine beside me is comforting. When one discovers that my eyes are open, that I'm really seeing things, he bellows "Hey Buddy!" so that all the other androids come running. Hey Buddy props me up and presses a button beside my head. The man in a white coat comes through the door, his soft, manicured hands clasped before his chest, eyes awash with hope and fear.

"Do you know who I am?" He asks me. He is so tall that even when he is sitting, he has to lean over to talk to me. The sound of his voice fills me with warmth and terror. I want to answer him, but find that I couldn't move my mouth or my head. "Of course," he says, as if I'd answered. "You can blink? Try once for no, twice for yes."

I blink twice. I think. He smiles warmly. "I'm going to check your body now, okay?" I blink again, twice, and try to turn my head to see if there is a mirror in the room. I want to see myself, though I can't think why, exactly. I also see that I'd been mistaken about the android nurses. Hey Buddy is fat, and the others are too plain to be inhuman.

Dr. Akachi places my hand on the bed beside me and asks if I am feeling any pain.

I blink once. I'm not feeling much of anything.

One day, I wake up from a dream of a boy with brown eyes and dark skin and think I have an idea of who he is. And somewhere in my bones, I feel that I was once very different. I tell one of the nurses about it, and she checks the screen beside me to make sure the cameras are still recording.

"What do you remember of the dream?" she asks. I tell her in the dream I am in a dark room with the boy, and he is holding a towel and telling me to get into the shower. He turns into a bird once I get into the shower, and then he flies out the window to get away from me. She makes notes on the vitals/screen by my head and asks me if I feel like the dream really happened. I don't know.

And that's how it goes for some time. My memory is somewhere between a dream that really happened and a movie playing in the next room. I can hear my past, sometimes, but I can never quite make out what I'm supposed to know about it. I was someone with a family and friends a long time ago.

One morning, Dr. Akachi brings me a hand mirror. A couple of muscled-up people in scrubs stand just inside the door, their faces inscrutable.

"Are they new nurses?" I ask. I am sitting in the chair, fully clothed, with three cameras trained on my face.

"Heavens, no," Dr. Akachi says, laughing. "They're old friends. They're here to make sure you feel safe and protected. That's why they're called orderlies. They keep the order." He turns back and the two orderlies nod at me. "Now, you want to see something beautiful?" Dr. Akachi hands me the mirror and I raise it slowly.

The face I see there is not one I recognize, but it's one I instantly like. There's a stately beak of a nose under brown/black, deep-set eyes. Just the barest bit of stubble along a square, thinly muscled jaw. My brown hair is short and shiny. I feel a real smile coming, and despite the cameras, I have this inexplicable feeling that I once knew this person and never thought I'd see him again. I *am* beautiful. I lower the mirror to look at Dr. Akachi, who is watching my face as though he might need to snap into action.

"How do you feel?" Dr. Akachi asks. I want to say something in particular, but my chest feels like its full of fingers.

Hey Buddy straps a heart-rate monitor to my chest as Dr. Akachi unfolds his work/screen. It's like the one I have used, but it's bigger and it hovers.

He touches the bottom and begins time-lapse footage of what he calls the "radical reorganization." He explains that the waving, naked girl in the tank is me.

"Or, maybe more like your sister, at this point." I watch her begin to dissolve as the pod shrinks and hardens. The meat of her limbs and torso go first, and then her bones, her teeth, layers of her skull. Over a matter of minutes, she has broken down into nothing but a brain, a tangle of nerves, and a throbbing, glowing set of lungs. Then, slowly, the goo of the girl's body begins to reconstitute itself until there is a longer, leaner, body in her place. My body.

"It took you 28 months to reorganize. You were 26 when you entered, and your body is 17 now."

THE FIRST THING I do when I get to the new house is to close all the blinds and excuse myself to take a shower. I haven't been alone since I woke up, and though I didn't care for a long time, I care now. Even though I know there's no real privacy anywhere, actual people don't follow me into the bathroom. I disrobe in front of the mirror and run my hands down the sides of my ribs, thighs, between my legs and toes. The hair on the back of my neck rises while I stand on one foot, and then the other. My skin is unblemished, soft as flower petals. I examine my teeth up close and find the row on the bottom looks like a sloppily constructed fence. My hair is fine and feathery, just beginning to grow in.

In the shower, I run cool water. I stay under the stream for a long time, breathing into lungs that were once Genevieve's and wondering what else of hers is still with me.

What is my name? is the question that I ask when I am dressed again and sitting on the couch beside Dr. Akachi. He looks up from his screen and tells one of the orderlies to check the camera in the hallway, which seems to be a little glitchy. The short one walks over to the wall and raises his hand. Beneath his palm, a soft light begins to glow.

The décor in the house is limited, but the furniture is plush and well made. Beneath my feet, the area rug is warm and velveteen. One wall is a *Window to Anywhere* style screen that is currently tuned to an English moor. I've been told that I'll be able to work with an interior decorator if I like, but I feel pretty happy with things as they are.

Dr. Akachi leans back on the couch and crosses his legs. He's no longer in a white coat, but is instead dressed in something that looks like a roomy grey flight suit. They're all wearing these outfits in different colors. New coolersuits, I am told. Indoor/outdoor. There are three hanging in my closet right now if I care to look.

"What do you feel about your name?" I am used to this kind of question by now. It doesn't bother me because it doesn't bother them when I don't have a good answer. Most of the time I am just confused or sad for no reason I can justify.

"I like Richard," I say.

Dr. Akachi smiles broadly and pats my shoulder. "Richard it is, then. How about a surname?" I think for a bit. The only surname I can think of is Akachi. I turn to the tall orderly with the dark skin. "What is your surname?"

"Locke," she says.

"Mine is Perlman," says the short one in the hallway. "But you can call me Mark."

I stand up and walk over to the bookshelves, where there are plenty of names to choose from. I pull a book from the middle shelf and see the outline of a body against a lonely road. "Faber," I say.

Locke takes the book from me and shows it to a camera somewhere above my head. "Richard Faber, then," she says, and puts the book back on the shelf. As she does, a loud noise explodes through the room and before I have a chance to react, both Locke and Mark have me sandwiched between their bodies. Over Mark's shoulder, I see Dr. Akachi fling open the door and run onto the porch. There is another loud noise, and Dr. Akachi falls backwards into the house, head hitting the stone floor with a crack, blood pooling. I try to push Locke away, but her grip is tight and her breath is even. She and Mark move me back into the bathroom and sit me down on the toilet lid. Mark disappears while Locke digs around in her pocket and produces a pocket knife. I try again to push her away but Mark comes back and closes the bathroom door behind her. He swallows hard. His breath is coming fast and sour in my face. Locke pulls a bottle of alcohol from the cabinet above my head and douses the knife. The alcohol hits my skin and nose in a cold splash, and suddenly, I find my voice enough to scream Dr. Akachi's name.

Locke looks at me like I am worthless and tells Mark to get me still. Mark lifts the bottom of my shirt up over my face and grabs both my hands.

"Listen, buddy," Locke says. "This is going to hurt for a bit, but you are not going to die." There is a second in which nobody breathes, and then I feel the blade of the knife pierce the skin at the top of my forearm and lay it open. I open my mouth, suck the fabric of my shirt through my teeth, and bear down against the pain until I see a flash of bright black-red.

When I wake, I'm still on the toilet and Mark is muttering about an artery while Locke is hastily stitching my arm. Blood covers everything. The cut runs from the base of my palm to the crease of my elbow and I feel a wave of nausea roll through my stomach and up through my chest. Little fireworks go off behind my eyelids and don't go away when I open my eyes. Mark's fingers open my mouth and force a pill onto my tongue.

"Swallow the pill," he says, holding a glass to my lips.

I fight another wave of nausea, and when I open my eyes again, he's gone. Locke wraps my arm tightly and tells Mark we're going to have to hope for the best. They stand me up and half drag me into an adjoining bedroom where they lay me down on a plastic-covered bed. Mark sticks a thick finger under the blinds and peers into the street. "Where is he?"

"On the way," says Locke. "Must be."

Blood is seeping through the makeshift tourniquet and I am just about to point this out when I hear the faint wail of a siren.

"I'm going to be sick," I tell them.

"Wait a minute," Locke says, reaching to cover my mouth. "Just hold it."

They hoist me up again and pull me through the back door, where a yellow EMS is waiting, lights and sirens going full blast. Locke and Mark load me up in the back and climb in after me. They strap me in and then hold on to the side bars while the driver careens through the neighborhood. I close my eyes slowly, but can still see all around me. I'm no longer nauseated, no longer afraid. I'm just watching Locke's beautiful smiling face hover over mine. I want to touch it, but I'm strapped in.

SOMEWHERE OUTSIDE THE city limits, we pull over into a dirt lot and park behind an abandoned mill. Locke and Mark help me out of the EMS and into a grey manual Honda that has seen better days. The driver of the EMS, now that I can see his face, looks familiar. He exchanges a few words with Locke, who takes the keys and gives him a hug. Mark shoots a little wave my way and they climb into the EMS.

The driver is short, built around the shoulders, and a little soft in the middle. His long-lashed eyes take up about half of his face.

"Is Dr. Akachi dead?" I ask him. He looks at me like he wants to touch me.

"Do you recognize me?"

I shrug. "You look familiar. But Dr. Akachi? Is he going to be all right?"

This time, he does touch my arm, as if to comfort. "I don't know if he's going to be all right," he says. "Let me see your wound." His fingers are practiced and gentle, and I feel no pain at all even though the bandage has soaked through with blood.

"I'm Eddie," he says, reaching into the back seat to retrieve a small red case full of first aid supplies. He lays a clean towel over the armrest and cuts through the blood-soaked bandage, letting out a low curse when he sees the damage. He glances up at me. "Don't look at this," he says, a dark little laugh escaping. "You're whiter than usual."

Maybe this is a joke, but I don't get it. I lean back against the headrest and try to think of nothing. Outside, it's a pale, close sky, and I wonder if it might rain. My body is uncomfortable, leaden, and I am suddenly overcome with a sadness so infinite that it feels as though my throat has been constricted. It's only tears. I lean my head against the cold glass of the window while Eddie's eyes are on my arm.

"Oh, hey," Eddie says quietly, his hands busy re-stitching Locke's hasty work. "What's your name?"

I don't answer while he swabs at the dried blood and applies a cream to the wound. He secures fresh bandages around my arm and lays it gently in my lap. Then he puts his arm around my shoulders and draws me close. I let him do this because I know I am lost.

Eddie smells of gasoline and tree bark. "I'm your friend," he says into my hair. "I've been your friend for a long, long time. You're safe. You hungry? Look back there." The seats are stained and patched, but in the back are two suitcases and a full bag of food. He removes a bag of chips and opens it. "These were your favorite." I accept one and a flavor explosion happens as soon as I bite down. I'm not sure if it's good or not, but it turns out I am very hungry and I eat the rest of the bag on my own.

Eddie pulls the Honda onto the highway and pats my leg. After I eat, I fall asleep again. When I wake up, it's dark and for a minute I think I'm back with Dr. Akachi and he's about to check my vitals. Then I move and there's a terrible pain running from my left hand all the way up to the base of my skull. Eddie pulls over to find another pill for me, and after a while, I've got that sweet feeling again.

"Richard," I tell him after we're back on the road. I have to search around for a bit for the second name. "Faber. Richard Faber."

"I'm Eddie Garza," Eddie says.

"Where are we going?"

"Somewhere safe. Up in the Blue Ridge Mountains."

"Tell me something I need to know," I say, not even sure about what to ask. "About me, or you? Or just anything."

"You look a lot like your mother," he says. "We've been friends since I was about 14. We were 14 together. Is this making any sense to you, or should I back up?"

I shake my head, but tell him to keep going anyway.

"We won't need coolersuits in Blue Ridge. The air is fine, and there are still regular seasons up there. We have friends, there, I guess, though you haven't met them. In your arm, there, that was where the tracking device had been implanted. I showed Locke what to do, but she panicked when she couldn't find it right away. I'm afraid you'll have a pretty big scar there."

"But it's out?"

"It's out. She showed it to me and I tossed it before we got out of the neighborhood."

"Why? Who's after me?"

Eddie laughs. "Well, nobody, we hope. But we couldn't take any chances."

"Is everyone dead?"

"No."

"Will I see them again?"

"I don't know."

I settle back into my seat and pull out another bag of chips. Eddie asks if I could grab him a bottle of water, so I open one for him.

"Why are you doing this?" I ask.

"I loved Genevieve."

Eddie pulls into a gas station and I get out to use the bathroom. In the mirror, I see what Eddie means about being white. I do see the ghost of someone familiar looking back, and whether it's my mother or Genevieve, I can't tell. I feel that teetering empty sadness begin to creep back, so I wash quickly and find Eddie out by the car. Now that I am standing, I see that I'm not much taller than him. He's dressed in a hoodie and boots, black hair curling around the backs of his ears. When he sees me approach, his face breaks into a relieved smile. In that moment, I know I once loved him.

I sleep most of the trip, though Eddie wakes me up to keep me hydrated and drugged. I cry some more against the window, which gets cooler every time I touch it. Trees line the highway. I can't see the sky first because of the trees and then because it's finally dark, and sometimes I feel Eddie's warm hand pass over my forehead or rest on my thigh. We arrive at the farm shortly after dawn has broken and as we pull onto the property, the trees give way to a glorious green clearing. At the far end is a gigantic wooden lodge and a barn, and there's a fast-moving fog rolling over the lake at the bottom of the valley.

"That's your benefactor," Eddie says as the lodge door opens and a short blonde man in a hooded t-shirt steps out onto the porch. I see a few people already out in the fields behind the barn, rows of leafy greens around their ankles. They turn their heads toward our car at once, like sunflowers sensing the sun, and where their faces should be are instead vast empty chasms.

Field Trip

KELLY ALMOST CALLED out on Saturday. It was not a good morning, but it was also not a *bad* morning; her bones were not heavier than her muscles could handle. She stood in front of the bathroom mirror for a while, trying to arrange her expression into something cheerful and patient. Failing that, she settled for benign and impassive, dotted some concealer beneath her eyes, and hoped for the best.

Overhead, the sky was already a hot, bright menace. Kelly pulled her sunglasses out of her bag and pushed her hair out of her face as she crossed the empty teacher lot. Don Bledsoe leaned against a short yellow bus in the shade.

"You're late," Don said, cradling a cup of hot coffee and pulling Kelly into a quick half-embrace. He wore his usual tailored jeans and dark vest, a messenger bag slung across his chest, driving cap tastefully angled over his forehead. "Gracious, I'm not ready for this," he said, watching two students tumble out of the backseat of a hotboxed Prius. "Do they not know we can *see* them?"

Eight art students showed, though fifteen had signed up. The low number was unsurprising. It was an early Saturday, a ninety-degree day in late November. A couple of the overachievers acted genuinely excited about an extra-curricular visit to a sculpture garden, but most of the students were in attendance to make up for excessive absences—same as Kelly. Every time she volunteered to drive the bus on a weekend, she earned back a personal day.

Kelly circled the bus, checked the tires, and then unlocked the door. Students climbed aboard in varying states of consciousness. Don Bledsoe settled in the back. Kelly adjusted the mirrors and walked the length of the bus, inspecting the seats and floor. Fernanda, a perpetually cheerful junior goth in Kelly's second period health class, held her hand high as Kelly passed. Kelly pulled a pack of gum from her pocket and gave it to Fernanda, who opened it and popped a piece in her mouth.

"Don't kill us, Kelly," Fernanda said, handing the pack of gum to the student behind her. Kelly caught her own reflection in the window above of an empty seat, her white cheek lit up like an unpeeled apple in the reflected sunlight, and resolved for the fifth time that week to give up carbs for good. And cigarettes.

Don leaned back against the window and put his feet up. He sipped his coffee thoughtfully and kept a steady eye on the students, asking them simple questions in either German or Latin. He refused to address any of his students in English, even outside of school, and as a result, he often had some of the best competitive foreign language students in the state. An accomplished local method actor and a scholar, a believer in consistency and practice, he commanded a healthy respect from his constituents.

It was an arid, two-hour ride to the sculpture garden. The installation, "Our Futures, Our Selves," was brand new, interactive, and promised to be a once-in-a-lifetime opportunity. Out west, the trees got shorter, the ground redder, and the buildings scarcer. The road off the highway, at once familiar to Kelly and locked away in some recessed memory, had been long forgotten by the state of Texas. Entire swaths of concrete were simply gone, replaced with caliche or rutted mud. By the time they pulled in to the parking lot, Kelly's mood had improved some, and the students all had a few more hours to sleep.

"Everybody up!" Kelly yelled, stretching her calves in little space at the front of the bus. Teenage limbs had spilled into the aisle between seats, suspended by fragile, snap-able tendons on imperfect hinges. They were all so breakable. She opened the door and stepped down into a dry, eternal wind. With nothing on the land to break it, the wind could feel like the sweeping hand of an invisible giant.

The little town where she'd spent most of her childhood was twenty miles further west; she'd brought a bunch of recalcitrant teens halfway home. Kelly's dad, long dead, had affectionately referred to her mother as cold-blooded, like the flat little lizards skittering between rocks in the back yard. Not because of any shared personality traits, but because she could happily adjust to any inhuman temperature West Texas had to offer, and she didn't need to eat much. She loved the feel of the wind around her bare ankles in the summer time.

Fernanda returned the half-empty pack of gum to Kelly in the bathroom of the Visitor's Center. From behind the locked stall door, Kelly caught some of the girls' gossip about one of the boys on the trip; Travis had come out as gay to one of them while simultaneously dating another, and there was some confusion as to whether this made him bisexual, gay, or just an opportunistic liar.

Don waited outside in the lobby. A permanent kind of tired had settled into his bones and put lines into his forehead. His mother was not quite dead from Parkinson's, and Don had recently moved in to be her full-time caretaker. He pulled a little bag of trail mix out of his pocket and offered to share. Kelly accepted a handful and they headed back toward the bus, where the students had loosely gathered to listen to a tour guide dressed in red and brown.

"Just follow the green arrows," Trudy the tour guide was saying, "and you can move at your own pace through the works." Her name was markered artfully upon the pocket of her uniform shirt. One of the boys began to saunter away from the group and Don cut him off with an offer of trail mix.

"These are interactive sculptures," Trudy continued, "and we encourage our visitors to touch the works, or climb them, or sit inside of them—whatever feels safe to you. Some pieces can be moved or reassembled. Create your own art! We want this experience to be memorable. Everyone will have a different experience here, and everyone should. Our guides are stationed around the grounds to answer questions, but we don't offer tours because you simply don't need one!"

Fernanda stood alone, hands jammed into the pockets of her black hoodie. Kelly walked over and stood next to her, motioning to another student, Ruby, to extract her earbuds and pay attention. When Trudy was finished, Kelly stepped onto the bus to shoo Travis out. He was a talented painter who asked to come on the trip and then tried to get out of it the day before. Kelly reassured him that he would have a good time, though she couldn't really be sure. She put her hand on his shoulder and felt scarecrow bones shifting beneath his shirt. The previous summer, Travis had locked himself into his room at the top of the stairs of his parents' McMansion and prison tattooed the first seven lines of Leonard Cohen's *Bird On A Wire* onto his left thigh. The infection had put him in the hospital for three days. He joined Ruby, who looked as though she had been forced off the bus at gunpoint.

The path to the garden wound down around a boulder perched tenuously on the side of a rocky outcrop that rose an easy hundred feet above their heads. The sculptures, Kelly thought, would need to be pretty impressive to hold their own against this landscape. As a child, she had been convinced that over every boulder, every rangy hill of dirt, the possibility of a new world existed.

The kids didn't speak to each other. They were all watching their feet, which were shod in fashionable and completely unsuitable shoes. Travis would be able to feel every single pebble through his cloth moccasins, but maybe that's exactly what he wanted. They'd all been asked to wear tennis shoes or hiking boots, and Fernanda had awakened that morning and chosen strappy sandals with slick leather bottoms.

Ruby stopped to dig her phone out of the pocket of her skinny jeans. Over her shoulder, Kelly watched her pass a finger over the screen and pull up a text box. Kelly tapped her on the shoulder and told her to put her phone away.

"I'm taking a picture," she said snottily, positioning the phone in front of her face. "These rocks are so fucking pretty."

"Text again and I'm taking the phone," Kelly whispered.

Ruby slid the phone back in her pocket and trotted ahead. She caught up with Travis, shoulder bumped him, and put an arm around his waist. He leaned in to her and they lowered their heads to talk.

Teaching was maybe not the best choice of profession for Kelly. She regarded Travis and Ruby with an uncomfortable mixture of boredom and jealousy and checked her watch to calculate the hours until they could get by with leaving. She hadn't considered being this close to home today. She hadn't prepared. Her mother seemed to think teaching was somehow beneath Kelly's true potential, that it was some kind of attempt to reverse engineer an unsatisfying growth into adulthood.

But teaching wasn't what her mother thought. She wasn't trying to recapture her youth by working with students who, each passing year, grew increasingly difficult to understand. She had no desire to be a friend. or role model, and had even ceased being interested in whether they learned anything in her classes. Her days were numbered. She knew that. But she *had* seen something there in the eyes of the ones who were growing into something they couldn't control. It was that. It was the helpless wilderness in their faces.

Her last year of high school, there was an accident. She hadn't seen the car coming, and the guardrail was compromised and she'd been mashed inside her mangled decade-old Buick for an hour while they pried at the doors with hammers and claws. While they called her name and reached for her hands through jagged holes in the glass, she wound her way back through the years of her life. There was only the lightness of her limbs and the sweet certainty of not having to face midterms. She pushed into that relief, found her way forward in a darkness that might have been frightening in a dream but only felt like home in experience.

Fifteen years on, that year of the accident was a resurfaced memory full of holes and flashes of nerves—the concussion on its own had left her stupid and dizzy for months afterward; the pain of re-teaching her left leg to hold weight again seemed better forgotten, anyway.

It was the first time she'd been rescued by strangers and not her own family, but she was soon delivered into the arms of her mother. She watched her legs return to pale pink health over the few years, dopily returning to those moments in the Buick when she might have escaped the rest of her life.

They climbed a short, steep incline and joined the others at the summit of what turned out to be the entrance of the park. Below them, the sculptures were so well positioned among the mesquites and deep limestone canyons that they didn't quite register as art. At the far side of the park, Kelly could make out the remnants of an old cattle fence. Beyond it was the rest of the world. Kelly thought about coming back alone sometime, just to follow that fence for a while and see how far it went into the brush. She knew she wouldn't, but for a moment, the conviction was strong and appealing. A few longhorns wandered around looking for green plants among the dirt, and there were two red-shirted guides sitting at stations on the far sides of the park. Other than those figures, the park was empty of movement. Don's group of students scrambled excitedly over the edge and spilled into the park. Kelly's group watched them disdainfully, and then looked at her.

"Do we have to do this?" Travis asked.

"What would you rather do?" Kelly asked Travis.

"We're done, right?" Ruby said, looking up from her phone. "There's the art. We saw it and everything. We could just go back to the bus and hang out now."

Fernanda stood beside them awkwardly. She knew that Ruby was not extending the invitation to her. Kelly shook her head. "We're going down there, and we're going to have fun." Travis grunted and picked at his left forearm. "And," Kelly continued, "you venture out of my sightline, you'll be sorry. That is a promise."

DON CAUGHT UP with Kelly beneath the armpit of a forty-foot-tall red giant whose bottom half was sunk below the surface of a brackish stock pond. He was standing in meager shade, watching the kids on the other side of the water. Fernanda had sullenly dogged Kelly's heels the entire way, but she was now standing at the edge of a larger group of kids engaged in a stone-throwing contest, feigning disinterest not two feet away from Travis.

"Well, today is turning out to be less torturous than I thought," Don said, placing a hand on the corrugated red tin of the giant's left forearm. "This place is pretty cool."

Kelly glanced around for Travis and Ruby, who were sitting under the arch of a hobbity structure comprised of permanently windswept-looking tree saplings. She ran a hand through her hair and felt dirt already gathering at the roots. She remembered the long baths of her childhood that required a strenuous tub scrubbing afterward.

"I grew up about an half from here," she told Don. He folded his arms and looked at her as though she'd been keeping a really fun secret from him.

"And I took you for a northerner! You must have burned up every summer with that complexion," he said, waving at her face.

"I stayed indoors, mostly," she said. "The sun is painful."

"We should take a little detour, don't you think? To the old homestead? We have to take these children to eat somewhere before we head back home."

"I haven't been back in so long," Kelly said.

"It's never too late to go looking for new regrets," Don said brightly, and wandered off toward the group of stone throwers. Kelly thought she might suggest her kids follow her to the maze constructed entirely of stacked newspapers. She turned back to Travis and Ruby and found them gone. Kelly circled the sapling structure twice, scanning the surrounding rocks.

"Did you see them take off?" she called to Fernanda, who was squatting at the stock pond, alone again, gazing at her reflection.

"Am I *supposed* to keep up with them?" Fernanda called back.

TRAVIS AND RUBY were standing under a leafy canopy, holding hands and gazing raptly at a large canvas hung between two trees. At their feet was a dewy carpet of fallen leaves. Kelly stepped through the makeshift gate and was immediately struck by the air, which was damp and breathable and cool. It was difficult to believe that the same sunlight filtering softly through the branches was responsible for punishing the grounds in the rest of the park. Kelly called to Travis, but her voice had no edge, no projection. Neither he nor Ruby seemed to hear her call or notice her presence. She took a deep breath and lush, sweet air lifted her irritation. A miracle. The fine layer of dust that had settled over her lips and eyelids now felt like an affront. She passed a hand over her face and wiped her hands on her jeans.

Canvases framed in dulled gilt were rigged up around the trees, facing every direction. The first one Kelly examined featured a complicated early-American village scene, full of children on their way to a parade. The streets were lined with buildings that could have been painted by Howard Finster, strangely crude in comparison to the living creatures on the road. Children fairly pulsated with light and life, so fine were their tiny expressions. The canvas next to it was the parade itself. Each face in the line of parading villagers was upturned, though some were concealed behind anachronistic carnival masks depicting wolves, elephants, alligators, and brightly twisted human mouths and chins. They all had those eyes that follow. It might have been creepy, but it was the best thing Kelly had seen all day.

"What the hell." Fernanda's curse was muted, carrying the resonance of words spoken inside a church. She was standing too close to Kelly, too close to the painting, her finger touching the face of a bald man. "This looks like Mr. Bledsoe," she said, pointing to a little man standing on an empty road adjacent to the parade. His hands were in his pockets and he was facing a large black beast with clubs for arms. The man in the painting did bear a strong resemblance to Don, but Don was a tall white man with a penchant for vests. He was not exactly one of a kind.

"Don't touch, Fernanda," Kelly said, batting her hand away from the little man.

"We've got to show him," Fernanda said. "He'll *love* this."

Kelly took another deep breath of damp air. The leaves were fairly glistening. "Are these trees part of the exhibit or what?"

"Look at Travis," Fernanda said. "He's standing up straight for the first time this quarter." Travis did look different. The color was high in his cheeks and lips as he gazed at the sky through the dense canopy. Nobody could save him from the rest of his life, she thought, looking at the faint scars that circled his forearms.

Kelly moved past Travis and stopped in front of a slick oil of a sunset that looked to be bleeding out. There was a person standing in a bay window at the back of a house. She held a mug of something warm, and she was long and straight and fair, her clothes and eyes paler shades of the blue and purple clouds.

"And that one looks like you," Fernanda said.

Painted into the reflection of the window was a faint figure—still and faceless and waiting just inside the treeline. Behind it, a green hillside covered in firs sloped toward a river. There was nothing all that familiar about the images, but Kelly was chilled by the expression that was not quite surfacing on the woman's face. Did she see that figure in the distance? Did she know it was coming for her? Kelly felt a damp warmth at the back of her neck, so different from anything she'd felt all day. Maybe it was the beginning of a fever.

Travis found himself next. His painting was propped up against a tree trunk—dark sky over dark sea, the only light in the frame falling on the shoulders of a handsome, anguished man. Here was a wilder, stronger version of Travis, shirtless, against the backdrop of a surfside bonfire blazing out of control.

Kelly felt a hand on her shoulder, and Fernanda nodded toward Ruby, a few paintings down. Before Kelly could say anything about the naked, bloodied figure of Ruby, a group of students tumbled in through the broken gate and were hushed by the atmosphere. She rushed toward Don.

"Keep your kids out," Kelly said, sure now that the man's upturned face in the painting was Don's. He gave her a puzzled look and gestured toward his group as though he had given up control long ago. Kelly looked past Don, down the hillside, and saw Trudy, shading her eyes with her left hand and gazing up at the group.

"We're all in here," she told Don, pointing at a branch just above his head. Swinging like a drugstore sign was a Victorian style portrait of Fernanda, minus her usual black leggings and spiderweb cloak. In the portrait, she looked a little younger, her eyes clouded over in white film. Fernanda gave a thumbs up in front of her portrait while Ruby took a picture with her phone.

"Oh my, where am I?" Don asked, gazing around the enclave. Kelly walked him over to the parade painting. "Is this what they meant by interactive?" Don asked, reaching for the dark animal facing his likeness. "Maybe it's just some cool face-recognition software. You know, like they use in haunted houses?"

"At any rate, it's disturbing. Parents are probably *already* calling the school. I can just feel it." Kelly began ordering students out of the exhibit, but word had spread and students were dashing from painting to painting, identifying each other and speculating about which deaths were most realistic.

Before them both, Travis stood in front of the painting of the woman in the bay window, his face serious, hands worrying the straps of his backpack.

"Is this your house?" he asked Kelly.

"No."

"I wonder why you're in the window, then."

"What are you looking at?" asked Fernanda, leaning in to the gilt frame. "In the window there, what are you looking at?"

Kelly sighed and opened her arms wide. "Time to go," she said, attempting to direct them toward the entrance again. "There's plenty more to see in the rest of the sculpture garden."

No one moved. The little enclave was now full, buzzing with the sound of low voices. The warmth at the back of her neck spread downward, and Kelly heard her name above all the other voices. Trudy, standing at the gate, beckoned her over.

"Are you in here?" she asked, nodding toward the middle of the exhibit.

Kelly shook her head, confused. "Am I supposed to be?"

Trudy shrugged and motioned for Kelly to follow. They left the damp, cool air behind and ventured back out into the wind. At first, the light against the limestone ridge made it painful to keep her eyes open, but as her pupils adjusted, Kelly could see that Trudy was leading her up stairs cut into the rocky ledge. They walked silently for a while, Trudy's walkie-talkie beeping and calling from her belt. From the summit, the sculptures below looked like natural outcrops of rusted steel and half-disintegrated animal bone.

"Let's just wait here for a minute." Trudy said, squaring her shoulders and resting her hands on her security belt. Kelly admired the sensible bun at her neck and the sharpness of her nose. She wondered where Trudy lived. In Kelly's old hometown, maybe. Below, there was a fifty-foot mobile made of recycled airplane engines. Kelly watched a propeller dip and float on a long piece of glinting steel.

"Did they all recognize themselves?" Trudy asked.

"Seemed to. How do you know who is coming to the park?"

"There," said Trudy, at once calming and instructive. She pointed toward the trees on the other side of the fence. It was moving toward them in the shadows of the twisted little mesquites, its featureless head like the cool underbelly of a crab. The tips of Kelly's fingers felt as though they had fallen asleep, so she raised them above her heart and crossed her arms. The pressure against her chest was comforting. Trudy moved a little closer to Kelly and rested a hand on her shoulder blade. "Nobody can save you from the rest of your life."

Tomorrow or Forever

THERE ARE THREE of us. Three of us on our backs on the trampoline, breathing in the heat and the sticky chlorine smell of post-pool skin. It's almost too hot to lie there, but it's the heat that holds me down.

"Our mothers must have liked being pregnant together," I say to the sky. Our mothers are the kind of sisters who talk on the phone every day. Avery comes up on an elbow and looks at me like I'm simple.

"Mike's adopted."

"I could be Jewish," Mike says. He rocks forward into a sitting position; his brown shoulders need a shirt or they will burn.

I know Mike is adopted. Everyone knows. It's not something we talk about much, but they expected Mike for a year the same way they expected me—and then a few months later, his mom was surprised to be pregnant with Avery. Because I have no idea what the human body is actually doing during gestation, I explain that pregnancy is merely a figure of speech, the nine-month anticipatory period of hope and dread. I like the story of Moses and hope that's how my own kid shows up one day. "Look," I say, "didn't they share the paint for our nurseries? Didn't they try to stop smoking for a while?"

"You're not really pregnant unless you drop the baby yourself," Avery tells me. Later, we head to the creek to look for rocks to sell. This is Mike's idea, not mine; I'm one hundred percent sure the folks in my neighborhood will not give us money for something from their own yard. But it's not like I have a better idea, and we are out of candy money. So we follow him down the back alley, past the swaying corn planted between my house and the highway. We've already been told that we can't get a ride to the Ski Lodge to swim today, and we have to stay around the neighborhood because last time we ventured into town, Mike flipped off a passing car and the driver recognized me and drove straight to our house. By the time we got home, my mother and the driver of the passing car (her co-teacher, Mrs. Blumley) were having coffee at the kitchen table and discussing the state of youth these days. We were separated the whole night, and there was no TV for any of us for almost a week.

The back alley is shaded. In the springtime and fall it smells of honeysuckle, but in the summer there's just the rotting food smell of people's trashcans left too long under the sun. We walk in a row, me in the middle. From the front, we maybe wouldn't even pass as family—my red hair and freckled skin, Avery's sharp chin and nose, Mike's round brown eyes and face. But we all three have the same short haircut for the summer, and from the back I imagine people might mistake us for triplets. As we walk, Avery picks things up. She is the youngest of us, but the bravest. She never spooks at a frog, never cries. Not for mother, father, animal.

Up ahead, Mike disappears in the brush down by the water. I grab Avery's bare arm. "I need to tell you something."

She stops for a second and I wait for her eyes to register the urgency in my face. I have practiced this face many times in the mirror. She raises her chin and pushes her blonde hair from her forehead, waiting for me to go on.

"I'm not who you think I am," I say.

"So what?" she says. Her skin shines dangerously feverish in the summer glare. I've been waiting to say this to somebody for weeks, but I'm momentarily confused by her answer.

"What do you mean, so what?" I ask her, but she is looking ahead for Mike. The sun makes bottle glass of her eyes.

"So what," she says again, but this time it's not a question.

Avery would make a good spy, the way she appears to not give a shit about even the most interesting of prospects. I watch her do this with Mike all the time. Even with her parents. She almost never gets the belt for this reason. Earlier that June, I'd been in the wrong place at the wrong time just as my father was turning to fill his first cup of coffee for the day. I'd been sleepily reaching for the box of powdered doughnuts, and as he turned toward me he accidentally sloshed the coffee over the plastic rim. It drenched his hand and soaked right though my t-shirt. After the ice bath, the blisters clustered into the shape of a watery cat that stretched over my left pectoral and down toward my navel. Dad's hand had to be wrapped for days afterward. My mother bought me four loose button-down Hawaiian shirts to go over the raised skin of the blisters along my chest. Alone, I wore no shirt, or I left it unbuttoned. I'd always been skinny—beaky, like my dad. I had no breasts to speak of, even though I'd been warned that puberty would soon make a girl of me. Then, a woman. I could not imagine what I'd look like in the future. I didn't try.

Once, I forgot to button up over the blister, even though I was in a public place. We'd been down at the Lodge. My father complained about paying Lodge dues every year, so he made it a point to take us to swim and eat cheap there at least twice a week. The Lodge is settled on a green hill overlooking Lake MacKenzie. It's two stories of the coldest AC I've ever felt, with a restaurant and porch that overlook the lake. One entire side of the Lodge is windows, and high school kids fight to get the window cleaning jobs every summer because they get to climb a two-story ladder and goof around at the top.

On the weekends in the summer and spring, the whole place turns into one big boating party. Kids go nuts all day in the pool, in the lake, at the ping pong tables, and at night their parents get drunk at the bar and stagger around all over the hill that slopes gently toward the lake, dancing under Christmas lights dangling from the limbs of trees. The regular high school kids who don't clean windows instead wait tables in the restaurant and smoke pot behind the dumpsters when they think no one's looking.

My dad figured that the upside to paying yearly dues was that he could recoup all that money in discount beers. We weren't water skiers, and we didn't even have a boat. We just used the pool and the restaurant. Out on the porch, though, you could eat while you watched the Talcum Ski Bee team practice barefoot tricks and complicated jumps on the lake. Even on days I hadn't been swimming, I looked forward to watching the skiers.

That night, we were waiting for my mother to meet us. The waitress asked my dad what his son would be having to drink. I froze, waiting for him to correct her. He always had, even when I'd been so little it didn't matter. My father let it pass this time, though, possibly out of embarrassment. Maybe I was too old for this kind of mistake. I'd crossed some invisible line. So I'd walked into the Lodge a girl, and walked out a boy. It was that simple.

This is what I want to tell Avery, but she is not looking at me anymore, and now the revelation seems absurd. She raises her hand and motions for quiet, like she has heard somebody behind us. My feet planted, I turn to see a mockingbird land in the branches of Mike's favorite pecan tree.

Mike can scale a tree in seconds if it has low-slung limbs and offers him a solid start. He started climbing young, way before he was smart enough to know when he should stop. He'd keep going, his toes gripping branches growing thinner and thinner. Against the winter sky, the bare branches looked like insides of lungs. Mike would go as high as he possibly could, and then he'd jump from a height too scary to be safe, claiming that his feet were lower down and had something like eyes all their own. My eyes are up here, he'd say, and my feet are down there. Big difference.

Their father had left when they were nine and ten years old, respectively. Nobody ever talked about why he moved to Houston and started buying them expensive presents. They lived with their mom in a salty red apartment building in Galveston, a few miles from the rocky beach.

I had mixed feelings about their dad, even though he was my uncle. They usually went from my house to his during the summer, and while I moped around on their last day in town, they got progressively manic until he showed up. His pointed boots beneath pressed blue jeans seemed threatening to me, like one swift kick might be lethal.

Mike emerges from the brush carrying something wrapped in a piece of cloth. When he sees us looking, he tries to hide it behind his back.

"Give it up," I say.

"It's mine." He backs up, twisting from Avery's reach. "I'm gonna sell it and buy us all something great."

I grab his shirt and threaten to pinch his nipple while Avery circles around and pries the object from his fingers. She kneels in the rocky dirt of the dry creek bed. It's a survival knife with a serrated edge so sharp it almost sings. At the base is a compass, suspended in an oily liquid. I want to touch the grip—a leathery looking surface stained with some kind of spill. Maybe blood. I reach for it, but Avery pulls it a couple of inches from my fingertips.

"Sell it?" I can't imagine why he'd want to sell something so useful. "Where'd you get that?" I asked.

"Nowhere," he says, narrowing his eyes. Mike's the kind of boy who loves a mystery. He has a magic set that he can't quite get the hang of.

Avery stands up and points the knife at his chest. "Show us where you found this," she says. Mike raises both hands in mock surrender. I push him a little bit closer to the knife. Just to see what she'll do. "Down by the fort. But Avery, man, it's ours. Finders keepers."

The fort is a neighborhood project that never stops. It's mostly been built by myself, Jeremy, and Dean, brothers from the end of my street. We're best friends during the year, but they're sent to camp up north every summer. This is actually good, as Jeremy and Dean think

Mike is dumber than a box of hair, and Avery once tried to strangle Dean when things got ugly over a game of Risk.

Jeremy and Dean left a month ago, so I don't know who has left the survival knife by the fort. Sometimes, though, when Jeremy and Dean and I escape to the fort on Mondays after school, we have to clear away crumpled beer cans and fast-food wrappers before we can start building or playing Alamo or whatever. It used to make me mad, the thought of other people using our fort at night. One time, I even set my alarm for midnight and snuck out on a Sunday to spy on them. I didn't see anything, but I heard plenty. Now, I just don't think about it. I close a door in my mind and the intruders disappear.

Avery walks the walls of the fort, checking all our hiding places. "Did you see anything else?"

The fort's ground level is a lean-to, built with twisted mesquite branches and abandoned doors. Dean's fifteen and strong. If you hit him at the right time, he'll still lead an awesome game of war around the fort, though I think those times are probably numbered. Dean's friend Ricky used to spend the weekends in our neighborhood with Dean and Jeremy. Ricky lived in one of those new neighborhoods with no trees. I'd been driving with my folks around his development, and the houses looked naked and vulnerable under their new dark shingles with nothing but little stick-like trunks drying up in brittle front yards. My neighborhood stays shady under a canopy of Live Oak, Sycamore, and Mimosa for most of the year.

We got the screen door and window frames from Ricky. Last spring, his dad drove us to a tear-down and helped load up an entire truck-bed full of scrap lumber and doors and windows, and then he drove it down the hill to the creek so we could build a second story up in the live oak branches. Under his tight white shirt, his muscles worked like spring-loaded pulleys. He never seemed to be tired. I couldn't decide what it was I felt, watching him lift himself up and over high branches using just the power of his arms. Lust? Jealousy?

He stopped coming in the spring when he started wrestling on the freshman team, and he'd been washing dishes at the Ski Lodge all summer to earn enough money for a wrestling camp in August. At first, I thought Dean was going to stop coming, too, but he helped us rig a trap door before he left for camp and swore he'd be able to trick Ricky into falling through it when he got back.

We climb the ladder nailed to the tree and sit in a circle around the knife. I've seen one like it at the hardware store, so I know it's worth three weeks of my allowance. Avery inspects the compass. She gives it an experimental twist and the whole thing pops off like the bottom of a flashlight. Inside the handle of the knife are a folded waterproof notebook, a pencil, a little tube of matches, and a folding fish hook attached to a string. She dumps the contents onto the plywood floor of the second story.

"We should test this stuff," Mike says, motioning toward the creek below us. "We should catch a fish, clean it, and cook it up."

"And then we should write it a letter?" Avery asks, flipping through the pages of the notebook.

"Yeah. The notebook is kind of stupid," I say.

"Unless you want to keep something secret," Mike says. Avery points out that the hidden compartment remained secret from us for about three minutes. "That's why you have to write in invisible ink," Mike says. He loads the survival gear into the handle again and drives the point into the bark by my head. Above us, a summer rainstorm blows through a mostly clear blue sky; fat, warm raindrops hit the tops of our heads and shoulders all the way home.

Back at the house while we're waiting for dinner, I haul a couple of stacks of *Cracked* magazines out of the closet and spread them out on the floor of my room. It feels a little weird to be inside while it's still light outside, but the strange bright rainstorm hasn't stopped and the air is soupy. Mike and I have taken off our wet t-shirts and replaced our wet cutoffs with dry ones. We are just about the same size and have always shared clothes. I usually start school in the fall with a couple pair of his jeans he's left behind.

Mike refuses to share his grape popsicle with me after he has promised to, and when I try to make him, he flings the whole drippy thing onto the carpet in my room and Avery has to cover for us with

Mom in the kitchen while we scrub the purple out of the shag fibers beside my bed. He calls me a stupid fucker because now nobody gets the popsicle at all. There is no way my mom will not notice the stain. We're pushing the bed against the wall to cover it up when Avery comes in and closes the door behind her.

"We are set for tomorrow," she says.

Mike does a standing jump from between the bed and the wall and rolls off the foot of the bed and onto the carpet. No trace of the stain. Avery retrieves the survival knife from my desk drawer and tosses it on the bed.

"Aunt Barbara said she'd get Uncle Brian to drop us off at the Lodge in the morning. We'll be right next to the lake all day. We've got till four." She digs her backpack out from under a pile of *Cracked* and throws her swimsuit inside.

Mike finds his own backpack and unzips the front pocket. His travel-size magic kit falls out.

I sit down on the bed. "I thought we were going to catch a fish in the creek," I say. A whole day alone at the Lodge? If I'd have asked my mother in the kitchen just now, I am certain she'd have said no. I never have luck with anything but long warnings and exasperated sighs in the kitchen. Sometimes I get a cabinet slam or two.

"Lake's better," says Mike. "The creek is filthy."

"I don't know," I say.

"Jesus, Jane, you're twelve years old now," Avery says. Then, nodding at my chest: "Not that anybody could tell."

I flex my muscles at her. "I look much older, I know."

"Not so much, weirdo," she says. "Button your shirt."

"Look, this is what I was trying to tell you earlier," I say. "I think I'm not who you think I am."

Mike looks up from the ball and cup trick he has set up on the floor. He squeezes one of the red foam balls between his thumb and forefinger. "Nobody is who you think."

NEXT MORNING, MIKE stuffs Fruit Rollups into our backpacks, alongside the towels and cutoffs, and my dad lets us ride in the bed of the pickup all the way to the Lodge. I lie down flat in the bed, and watch the tops of cable lines rise and fall between the poles. Mike catches his hat before it blows off his head and onto Kingsbury Street. We eat the Fruit Rollups on the way, wordlessly assuring one another that we'll soon be feasting on fresh catfish.

Avery's got the knife in her bag. There was a little argument about who got to carry what just before we left, but Mike settled down when Avery said he could have it on the way back.

Dad drops us off at the Lodge and promises to be back at four, when happy hour starts. Not many people are around, but I spot Ricky in his white apron at the door of the restaurant. I hesitate, then decide not to say anything to him. The sky looks threatening again.

The lake is high because for once we've had plenty of rain this spring and summer. Most Julys start brown and get browner, but this summer, there is a different shade of green everywhere you look. Caladiums billow like Viking sails. Ivy drops heavy vines. The trees will add a lovely fat ring to their under-bark timelines.

We pass the restaurant on the way down to the lake. Ricky's standing outside on the steps of the deck, smoking, and we can't avoid him. When he sees us, he smiles and waves us over. Sometimes he acts like he doesn't know me when I'm there for dinner, so I'm a little surprised. "My cousins," I say, pointing at Avery and Mike. He offers them cigarettes, but Mike shakes his head and darts off down the hill toward the water.

"We came to fish," Avery says.

"Don't mean you can't join me for a smoke," Ricky answers, exhaling out the side of his mouth. I can't believe he's smoking. It can't be good for wrestling. To my complete astonishment, Avery shrugs and reaches for his half-gone cigarette. She drags deeply as Ricky lights another for himself.

"Ricky's Dean's best friend," I tell Avery, hoping she will hate him by association and throw the cigarette away. Instead, she gives him half a smile and turns toward the water.

"You don't smoke," I say when we're halfway down the hill.

"Shut up, Jane," she answers.

Scattered over the hill are several concrete picnic tables and charcoal grills. We spread our blanket on the bank under the trees, where no one can see us. Avery throws the still burning cigarette into the lake and breaks off a long slender sycamore branch. She notches the end for the fishing line, which she finishes off with some kind of fancy knot I've never seen before. Mike digs for bait in the wet dirt.

"I've got something!" he yells. Over his shoulder, I can see that he's come across a fat white grub. He doesn't touch it.

"Mother of God," says Avery. She threads the grub and slings it into the water. "Keep digging," she tells Mike. "We need more."

Though it's still early and we're under the trees, before long we are sweaty, dirty, and hungry. We lose grub after grub to sneaky catfish. Mike strips and heads for the lake to cool off, but I stop him from going in and scaring the fish. He dips a toe in anyway.

"Let's call home. We're going to starve to death before Uncle Brian comes back."

"This is why they call it fishing," Avery says. "Not catching."

"Patience!" I say, though I'm edging toward a full blown foul mood myself. I look up toward the Lodge. There's nobody around, and I'm buoyed by the memory of the possibility of being taken for a boy again, the lake and the Lodge providing temporary cover from my real life. I take off my shirt and lean up against the trunk of a smooth white sycamore. It's cool against my shoulder blades. The coffee-burn scar is less and less of a surprise to me every time I see it. I kind of like the tautness of the new skin.

Mike sits down beside me and pulls his magic kit out. He shuffles a deck and asks me to choose a card, any card. He misses the first four times, but on the fifth, he gets my card right. I'm so surprised, I look up to tell Avery, but at that moment, she lets out a whoop and drags a nine- inch catfish onto the bank of the lake. She catches it under the fins the way our grandfather showed us, and lets it flop around in her hand.

Mike grabs my shirt, wraps the fish up, and turns to me with a grin. We gather our backpacks and run to the first picnic table on the hill. Avery pulls out the knife and inserts the shining tip into the anus of the fish. As she slices upward toward the head, she almost punctures the base of her thumb.

"Hold it underneath," I remind her.

"I know!" Avery slams the fish down onto the concrete tabletop, and a little bit of stomach slides out. She makes a few incisions just under the head of the fish, and strips the fins off the back and sides. Just as she is pulling the head back to skin it, I realize we have no way to cook it.

"Shit," I say. "Do you think the restaurant has charcoal?"

Avery stops, her knife in mid-air. Her face falls. "Oh man. And lighter fluid."

"Nice," Mike says, looking at me. "I brought the Fruit Rollups," he says. My stomach growls. I look at the fish half gutted, and know I don't really want to eat it anymore. Mike volunteers to find Ricky and ask him about grilling supplies. Avery finishes off the fish, and we sit down to wait. I know the fish won't stay good for long, even though the sun is behind the clouds.

"Put your shirt on. You're not a boy," Avery says.

"Don't be an asshole," I say. She's never cared before.

"I'm just realistic."

"You think there's no way that I could be different? Grow up different than what you think?"

"Please. You can't keep believing in things that won't happen. Tomorrow you're gonna wake up and you won't be a tomboy anymore. That's what my mom says happened to her."

I think that's a lie. I've seen pictures of my Aunt Gerri as a child, her hair in finger waves, feet in saddle shoes. So she scraped up her knees in a few ancient bike accidents. She's nothing like me.

"You don't know anything," I say. I feel her turn to look at me, but I don't look back. Instead, I squint at the looming thunderheads. A few rain drops hit the cement table top.

"I know they put kids in the hospital for *acting out*. Or you have to go to military school or something. Just stop thinking about it."

She's not talking about me anymore. Or to me. I sigh. "Once you're thirteen you don't have to go to Houston anymore. You can choose. My mom said."

Avery's laugh is terrible. "She's pregnant."

"Your mom?"

"The stepmother."

"Why didn't you tell me?" I ask.

"Sometimes I'm stupid as you," she says.

MIKE RETURNS WITH nothing, but says Ricky has barbeque supplies in his car out back, and we can go out there and pick up what they need on his break in twenty minutes.

I eye the fish. "You think it'll stay good?"

"We'll make Mike taste it first," Avery says. He's already down by the water again, jumping for the lowest limb of a thick pecan tree. I root through her backpack for another t-shirt, and put it on.

"Let's just go," Avery picks up her backpack, and we head toward the Lodge.

"It's early for a break," Ricky says, "but I could use a little walk. It's so boring, prepping alone." The kitchen is empty. On the long counter against the wall are tons of onions and tomatoes waiting to be chopped into pico de gallo, or salsa, or something. There's a window right above the counter so that the guests can watch what's going on in the kitchen.

"We found something really cool at the fort," I tell Ricky. He looks slightly embarrassed and falls in right beside Avery and explains that he's not supposed to open alone. He's supposed to have a prep partner, but she's called in sick. "More like hungover," he says. "What kind of fish you get?"

"Catfish," Avery says.

"A big one."

"Thanks for letting us use your stuff," Avery says. A green Rabbit is parked by itself on the other side of the lot. The rain is holding off, but the air is so thick I think it might feel nice to have gills. Ricky unlocks the trunk. He locates a half-empty bag of charcoal under the heaps of empty beer cans and hefts it into my arms. I stagger under the weight. Avery takes her backpack off and trades it for the bag of charcoal. Ricky hands me a can of lighter fluid and a box of matches, so I put those into the backpack and follow them back toward the kitchen.

Ricky holds the door open for us. He smells of greasy hair product, the kind that leaves the bottom of your bathtub slick when you try to shampoo it out. I catch his eyes as I'm passing, and a small lump forms in the pit of my stomach.

Avery pauses to put the charcoal down for a minute in the middle of the kitchen. I wonder briefly why Ricky didn't carry the heavy bag, but that thought seems a little bit sexist, so I close the door on it.

"Why don't you give us a minute, okay?" Ricky looks at me. I stop. A minute for what? I look back at Avery; she's trying to get the bag over her left shoulder like a sack of potatoes.

"Our fish will go bad if we don't get it on the grill," I say. Ricky smiles at me. I think it's the first time he's really addressed me directly.

"It's all right, man," he says. "We're just going to talk a little. You know how it is."

I don't know how it is. "Avery's twelve. She acts like a smartass, but she's only twelve."

Avery gives up on the shoulder bit and just rolls up the top to use as a handle. She walks up and demands I trade backpack for charcoal again.

"Let's get out of here," I say, and start to grab her hand to pull her away from Ricky. He steps back, as if stung.

"Hey. I'm not a creep," he says.

"Whatever," I say, "we're going."

"Nice thank you."

Avery pulls her hand from mine and shoots me the same kind of look my mother gives me when I've just done something embarrassing in public. Some mix of shame and hopelessness about the way I turned out.

We carry the backpack and charcoal out to the picnic table where Mike is waiting with the matches from the secret compartment in the knife. I don't tell her about Ricky's request. I'm mad about that look. We stack the coals, spray them down with lighter fluid, and watch the blaze for a few silent minutes. I'm not sure what I would have done had Ricky insisted he get some alone time with Avery. He's stronger than Mike and me. Stronger than Avery. I'm mulling this over when I see him heading down the hill toward us, bright white apron flapping at his shins.

"How's the barbeque, kids?" he asks, setting down a metal platter and a pair of tongs. When he smiles, his eyes and teeth are brilliant as his apron. Against the looming thunderheads, he seems illuminated from within. He slides the fish onto the platter.

"It's gonna be a while," Mike says.

"Unless you want it Cajun," Ricky replies, pulling a small cylinder of a dark spice from his pocket. He offers it to Avery, who takes the spice and considers it.

"There's no label," she says.

"It should be labeled 'delicious,'" Ricky answers. Mike, oblivious, grabs the spice from her hands and shakes it in front of his own face. Panic surges from my stomach to my lungs, and I imagine the upside-down trees in my chest blooming suddenly and violently. Ricky snatches the spice back from Mike, unscrews the top, and shakes a good amount onto both sides of our catfish.

"Jesus, Ricky," I say. "That's our fish." Ricky doesn't respond. He lifts the fish from the platter and lays it on the grill, just at the edge of the flame. I don't know whether to give in or fight, so I do something that is neither. I awkwardly insert my body into the space between them as Ricky tries to sidle closer to Avery.

"So where do you go to school?" he asks, pushing me aside and closing in tight. Avery backs up, away from the grill, away from him.

"Enough," I tell him.

Without taking his eye off Avery, Ricky says, "You both might want to step away from the fish."

I look over at the grill, and the fish is sizzling, popping. Sparks are flying from the tail, the end nearest to the open flame. Mike's between me and the grill, so I grab his arm and pull him toward me just as the fish blows. A chunk of charred flesh hits me hard in the neck, and I stumble backwards, trying to push Mike upright. He falls on top of me anyway. I turn my face to avoid his elbow. From the ground, I see Ricky on top of Avery in a similar manner, though I doubt it's accidental.

I shove Mike off my chest and scramble over to Ricky, who is laughing over Avery's face. I step back and deliver a solid kick to his ribs, forcing him to roll off her body and onto his back. "Get up!" I shout, fists ready. "Get up, creep!"

"What the fuck is your problem, Jane?" Avery is in my face, her cheeks enflamed and swollen. Again, that look. That terrible look. She kneels again at Ricky's side; he's mewling and clutching his side and breathing raggedly.

"Oh, come on," I say. "He can get up."

Mike joins me, picking bits of fish out of his hair. "Gunpowder," he says. "Brilliant."

Troglodytes

THERE WAS ONLY one job opening in her father's department at Ethel Smalls, and Julia wasn't picky. After an interview and quick orientation, her new supervisor handed her a box and led her out to the floor where the rest of the Articulation Specialists hunched beneath fluorescent lights. It was a large room, chilly and quiet. They found her mentor, Pete, in a sea of shoulders and backs. He was a small pale guy, anxiety riding his prematurely balding forehead. His handshake was friendly.

"Meet Milton," Pete said, nodding at four neat rows of bones. He handed Julia a pair of gloves and she took off her jewelry while Pete explained the process of cleaning, sorting, labeling, and re-storing the bones in airtight bags. JoAllen Primates, a private company, provided the university with a steady flow of chimpanzee bones, which the university kept as a research collection to study primate functional morphology and evolution. He pointed at the enormous shelf that ran along one side of the old dining hall.

"Barbras and Miltons are females and males over thirty. Joeys and Rachels are all twenty-nine and younger. When you're done, you separate them by age and sex and stick them on the shelf." Pete took off his glasses and rubbed the bridge of his nose. He had a slight stutter, just a shadow of hesitation before soft vowel sounds. "Any questions so far?"

Julia shook her head. Pete disappeared behind the large shelf, came back, and handed Julia her own skeletal map and a stack of actual-size photographs to help with identification of smaller bones. He stood over Julia as she lifted the lid on her first Barbra, a jumble of pearly yellow bones, weighty and smooth. Julia set Barbra's heavy cranium on top of the box and looked at it while she wiped oozing lipids from the chimp's lower vertebrae. When they were clean, she tried to remember how to line them up. She glanced at the information on the box, stalling. Barbra had died the year she was born.

"Devil's in the details," Pete told her, reaching across the table to flip through the laminated photos. He pulled four or five from the stack and placed them in front of her, beside their respective bones. His hands were neat and quick as hummingbirds.

"How long you been here?" Julia asked him.

Pete sat back and sighed. "God. Too long."

After work, Pete invited her out back for a smoke. In the alley behind the building, a tall black girl raised her hand in greeting and introduced herself as Betty. "I'm trying to quit, you know," she said, shaking a cigarette from the soft pack in her shirt pocket. She handed one to Julia.

"Yeah, me too, actually," said Julia, even though it was a lie. She'd just learned how to inhale.

"Pete's a bad influence." Betty winked at Julia.

"So what happens to the bones?" Julia asked. She'd experienced a pang of concern just before putting her first Barbra on the list of catalogued skeletons.

Betty lit her cigarette off the end of Pete's. She was slight and shaped like a question mark, as though she'd been doing this work for years. Several hairs shone white against her dark ponytail in the lamplight. "Who knows?" Betty said.

"They sell them to universities," Pete said. "It's no mystery."

"You don't know that," Betty said sharply.

"Well, what else are they gonna do?"

"I don't know, Pete. You don't either." Julia wondered if they were still talking about the bones. "It's a private company," Betty said, turning back to Julia, "and they don't tell us shit."

Julia walked home, thinking about Barbra's last day on earth, which very well could have been Julia's first. A horrible vision of opening mouths—her first breath, Barbra's last—came to her just as she stepped inside the front hallway of her parents' house.

Julia ate lunch every day after that with Betty and Pete, who enjoyed an unbalanced intimacy Julia thought might have been the product of couple-hood gone to pasture. It was hard to tell, until she found them whisper-fighting in the alley on Friday evening, unlit cigarettes in one hand, lighters in the other.

"We're trying to be friends," Pete told Julia after Betty had walked away.

"Is it working?" Julia asked. Betty hadn't even said goodbye.

"I can't tell," Pete said, shrugging. "So, what's going on this weekend?" He leaned awkwardly against the wheelchair railing.

Julia shrugged and pulled her backpack onto her shoulder. "Oh, I don't know," she said. "Stuff." She hoped Pete wasn't fishing for information. She wasn't interested in divulging anything personal, even though her weekend forecast was bleak. It most likely involved a labor-intensive but ultimately futile project of her mother's: last weekend she had hemmed and hung new curtains in every room in the house only to come home after work on Monday to find an interior designer at the kitchen table with books full of window treatments. She'd been incensed. Then, magically, halfway through the den, she didn't care. She instead walked to her bedroom, which held the last hard yellow light of the day. The curtains in this room were untouched; she pushed one panel aside and looked across the lawn. Gary was home. She supposed he was still looking for a job. Some evenings, she could see his long shadow in the front windows as he set the dining room table.

Julia had known Gary for most of her life, so she married him when he asked. Six months later, she woke up one morning feeling certain that she didn't want to know him any longer. The next day, Julia was back in her childhood bedroom, staring at the ceiling and trying to think of what to do next.

Her father had pulled some strings at the university to get her the chimp job, insisting it was just the thing to get her back on track. This was this kind of reassuring talk that kept her from succumbing to a sudden dark suspicion that her life was somehow close to an end. She wasn't depressed about Gary, or her last job, which had ended as badly as the marriage. It was just impossible to keep the reckless machines of memory from shifting into high gear when she thought about her future. She couldn't imagine any other life than her own, and when she did, it was only from that day backwards. It wasn't something she talked about.

Pete said, "We could go to a movie. Your choice."

Julia smiled and said maybe some other time.

Julia's second week brought her a Joey, a young chimp with a badly healed break in his left arm. She separated his ribs and lined them up, placed his pelvis below. She was speeding through a chimp and a half per day now, and didn't need the cards much anymore. But she enjoyed Pete's company and insisted, when her supervisor asked, that she wasn't ready for her own table. The Joey was small, and his bones felt winning and sweet beneath her hands. She hated to drop him into the bleach, and almost said so to Pete. She finished sorting and labeling an hour before closing, and spent the rest of the time in the back alley with Betty and Pete, who seemed trapped together at the bottom of a well.

That night she dreamed of the Joey: lips taut with pain, his mother laying fruit near his mouth and worrying through the hair on his chest. White-hot light behind his body hurt her eyes, and Julia woke up shivering even though it was warm beneath her bedcovers, and even warmer in her dream. She dressed and got to work early, took the Joey down, and dumped his bones on the table. She laid him out in the position of her dream and felt like reaching through the table, into some space other than the one she could see. She wondered if she was crazy. Then she put his crooked humerus in her backpack and the rest of him back on the shelf.

Julia was already cleaning another Barbra when Pete walked in the door, a shiny green-purple bruise covering most of his left eye and cheek.

"I know what you're thinking," he said, pointing at the swollen side of his face. He looked older somehow, brimming with something unidentifiable.

How could he know what she was thinking? "A rumble?" she asked.

He smiled at her and shook his head. "So much better," he said. Pete uncovered his first chimp and started working. Every once in a while, she saw him reach up and touch the tight skin over his unshaven cheekbone.

"The weirdness is over," Betty told Julia on the way to lunch. "You know, between Pete and me? It's over."

"Are you limping?" Julia asked.

"There's this game in Drake Park," Betty said, uncapping her cottage cheese. Betty always brought the same thing to eat: two boiled eggs and a cup of cottage cheese.

Pete tossed his bag lunch on the table next to Betty. "It's not a game," he said, opening the refrigerator. "It's a fight."

Julia was surprised. Betty and Pete didn't seem like the Ren-Fair type. She'd seen the fights—folks dressed in seventeenth-century garb, chasing each other with wooden swords wrapped in bed sheets.

"Did Betty do that to you?" Julia asked, pointing at Pete's eye.

Pete smiled and sat down. Betty grabbed his chin and planted a kiss on his good cheek.

"Do you want to come this weekend?" he asked. "It sounds hokey, but you just have to see it." Betty scooped some cottage cheese onto a slice of egg and ate it, her eyes suddenly hard. Julia said she would pass. She opened her backpack and reached for some change, wondering if she would beat the shit out of Gary if she had the chance. Her fingers closed around the Joey's forearm. She blushed.

When she got home, she put the Joey's bone in her top drawer. Her father grilled kabobs. The zucchini tasted like old pennies. When he asked about Gary, she answered honestly that she didn't miss him at all.

At night, she dreamed of the chimps. Births and fruit and fights. She stole a bone every day or so, carried it around for a while, then put it in the top drawer of her dresser, with the others.

Gary respected her privacy for exactly one month, which is what Julia had asked him to do. He called on the third of March and spoke to her mother, who was unable to hide her relief at the sound of his voice. She stepped over the piles of water damaged books she had purchased at a yard sale—she was planning to decoupage the kitchen counters—and handed the phone to Julia. The yellow cord vibrated.

"You said a month," Gary said.

"I did."

"Do you want to come over?"

"That's okay," she said, standing to look out the side window. She could see him. She had worn that blue shirt of his more than he had.

"No, Julia, nothing is *okay*. I want to see you."

"Look out your window," she said. He lifted his head and she could see his eyes narrow angrily. She waved.

"Fuck you," he said, and hung up.

Julia handed the phone back to her mother and excused herself.

"I wish you would just quit this mess," her mother said, but Julia was already in the hallway.

The top drawer was heavy. She picked up a handful of bones, some creamy, ivory soft, some chipped and brittle as china. She thought she could remember each chimp clearly, and thought perhaps this was the reason Pete had warned her about inappropriate attachment. Julia put the bones back in the drawer, went out to her father's workshop, and stole fishing line, and the dremel. She spent the rest of the evening and most of the night articulating the pieces of her chimp. The bones were beautiful against one another. After a few hours of sleep, she awoke, excited for the first time to get to work.

Pete and Betty continued to arrive at work looking as if they had just stepped from the boxing ring. The worse their condition, the happier they seemed.

"Fight's tonight," Betty told Julia one evening as they smoked in the back alley. The days were getting longer. "You want to come?"

Julia wanted to pin Betty's shoulders back against the building, straighten her up. "Do you want me to?" She felt sure that Betty did not want her there.

"You can just watch," Betty said. "You don't have to do anything."

"Pete asked me out last week," Julia said. "I thought I should tell you."

Betty inhaled sharply, shaking her head. "Pete's gay," she said.

"You're not a couple?"

"We were once, but that was when Pete was a woman. And now that he's a man, he's only interested in men. Isn't that something." Betty's tone suggested that it was *not* something; it was everything. "So there's no way he's into you."

"We were standing right here," Julia said, more offended that Betty didn't believe her than she was surprised about Pete's past. "He said 'movie, your choice.' He was all stuttery."

"Well, you misunderstood," said Betty. She ground the cigarette butt out on the side of the building. "Drake Park, seven thirty."

When Julia got home, she found Gary and his folks camped out in her den. He'd cut his hair bootcamp short, and was wearing a pair of dark, fitted jeans she'd never seen before. She could smell grilled meat. Gary unfolded himself from the couch and started toward her just as her father swung through the kitchen door with a platter piled high with brisket. It was something they had done all her life, the two families, before Gary and Julia were married. They ate barbeque and watched network television during desert and then Julia and Gary snuck off to the basement where they turned on the same program and had sex on the couch. Only they didn't have to sneak, not really. By their sophomore year in high school, Gary's mother had already given Gary her grandmother's ring. Julia's mother had the ring resized by the time they had chosen a college and apartment next to campus—a pretty little diamond in big platinum prongs.

"Just like old times!" Julia's father set the platter on the dining room table between the potato salad and baked beans and began untying his apron.

"I can't stay," Julia said to all of them, to no one in particular. "I have plans." She backed through the hallway and out the front door. Gary was fast, out on the lawn in front of her before she hit the sidewalk.

"I'm supposed to be somewhere," Julia said.

"Is it Dallas?" Gary asked quietly, letting her pass. "I told you. It's all over, all done with."

"My life—" She wanted to say *is over*, but instead she said "is complicated."

It was too early for the fight at Drake Park. Julia found a bench in front of the water and pretended to read a book while the dog walkers passed. She tried to picture Pete, small and nervous, as a woman. She couldn't, but wondered about his family, what they had called him before he was Pete. The sun was hanging low in the trees on the far side of the park. She tried to think about where she should go after the fight, but found her options limited, and distasteful. Any time she focused on her future self, her mind darkened to a pinhole of light, the center of a still-hot television screen. She took a deep breath, rooted herself on the bench, and tried to wipe her mind of expectation. Thoughts about the chimps came easier, and she reached into her backpack to find a Barbra's lower third lumbar. She felt better, almost instantly.

Around seven o'clock, people started arriving for the fight. A muscular man in a maroon tunic and matching boots opened a large duffel bag and began handing weapons to three others, smaller than him but in similar dress. Julia guessed they were a team. The big guy swung his sword for a while, then picked up a mace.

Pete and Betty arrived during the warm-up. Julia hung back and watched them approach; they were dressed from head to foot in white tennis gear. From his Wilson racket bag, Pete withdrew two wooden swords, their blades wrapped tightly in a brilliant blue material.

A big archer with cascading blonde curls loaded up an arrow wrapped in foam and let it fly at Betty, who easily deflected it. She adjusted her visor, picked up her shield, and stepped into line with Pete. At seven-thirty, the archer shot an arrow straight up into the air and shouted "Carry on!" And everybody charged everybody else. Julia had a hard time figuring out the teams, though Pete and Betty pointed their swords away from each other. The first fight ended quickly, with victims dropping their weapons after the first and second blow, and then taking themselves out of the game after the third. A cheer went up for the big guy in maroon, who was the last one standing, and then the teams realigned themselves, the arrow went up, and they charged each other again.

Several costumes on the field seemed to hinder performance, but Pete and Betty were agile as cats, working back to back as a team, laying folks out. After a few fights, Julia realized that one of the teams was shrinking—each time a fight ended, the losing team forfeited a player to the other side. The fighter had to switch, to turn on his or her home team and fight for the bigger team. There were no POWs.

JULIA AND GARY had been married only a few months when Gary introduced the Dallas idea. He was gentle, but firm, and insisted that it would not affect their love for one another. A couple of trips a year, at most. And she was free to join if she felt so inclined. He held her close while she cried into his chest.

"Nobody has to know," he told her.

"I will know."

"How about we do it together, then? We've always done everything together."

"I only want to be with you. What is wrong with just me?"

So they went to Dallas for a weekend, and met up at the Cedar Ridge Bed and Breakfast where there were other couples, young and smart and willing to make the effort. They played harmless college drinking games in front of the fireplace downstairs. Slowly, couples began separating and disappearing into different rooms of the house. Gary was led away by a dark-haired woman who was a bit taller than him. Julia tucked her feet beneath her on the couch and sipped her vodka tonic, hoping to soon be so drunk she could forget what Gary was doing only a closed door away.

She asked for drink after drink until a red-headed man who smelled of sandpaper leaned her against the back of the couch and began to unbuckle his belt. She closed her eyes and kept them closed until she was back in the car with Gary the next morning. He was happy, he said. His happiness sailed them all the way home.

After that, it was harder to say no, impossible to explain away her reluctance to embrace what Gary called the natural state of human sexuality. Men needed women. Women needed men. Couples fared better than single men in the scene. The stats bore him out. The science was there, along with thousands of articles and sites that detailed the richness of relationships in which both partners could explore their sexual selves together. No threat of cheating, no miscommunication, no more puritanical expectations of lifetime monogamy.

Gary bought books that they read together in bed. He brought flowers to her work. They cooked and talked and had sex and then once a month, booked a room at the B&B in Dallas. It wasn't that the Dallas folks weren't nice. They were kind and funny, clear-eyed about the futures their decisions would provide. In comparison, Julia felt like a prude, and made sure she drank enough each time to ensure that no one else would think she wanted to be anywhere other than Cedar Ridge.

BETTY WAS NEVER the last one standing; every time it got close, she seemed to throw her win at the last minute. Eventually, when only a few people were left, she was forfeited to the other team. She gave Pete a look, turned around, waited for the signal, and then rushed him as though he were the only one on the field. He was waiting behind the wooden shield, his sword jutting from the middle of his body. Betty faked high, then swung at his feet, and as the fight died down around them, people sat back on their heels to watch. They fought so closely that the edge of Betty's shield caught the tip of Pete's nose. She regrouped and turned back on him, slowing only when she noticed the bright red blood striping his polo. Pete brought his hand to his face and smiled. He jogged backward a few feet, slowly separating his sword and shield, exposing his body in a manner Julia found vaguely unsettling. Betty charged again and he sidestepped her, catching the back of her calf as she passed. She threw down her shield and beckoned him with her sword. She let him get close, then cleanly whipped the sword from his hand and smacked his bare shoulder with the flat edge of her wooden blade. As he grabbed his shoulder, Betty circled around to his bare side and drove the butt of her sword into his ribs.

He crouched, curled into a ball on the grass. Betty bent over him, breathing hard. Julia grabbed her backpack and ran across the field, sure Pete's ribs were broken. She knelt beside him. "I'll go," she told him. "Let's go to a movie."

"A movie?" Pete raised his head and waved Betty off. "Now?"

Julia looked at Betty, who stood adjusting her wristband, pretending not to hear their conversation. "Now," Julia said. "I don't live far. We'll clean you up." She held out her hand, he took it, and she helped him off the field and three blocks south to the street where her parents lived.

"Why'd you change your mind?" Pete asked, holding his side and trying not to limp.

"Why do you and Betty fuck each other up so bad? What's that about?"

"My question first."

Julia didn't answer.

"She's angry," Pete said, finally.

"*She's* angry?"

Pete laughed weakly, wincing. "I guess I am, too."

"Nice. Don't bring your sword to the movies."

Pete was leaning on her heavily by the time they reached the house. His nose was bleeding again. "So why'd you say yes?"

She opened the door and led him into the den. Her parents and their guests looked up from slices of key lime pie.

"Hey guys," she said, over the sound of a car commercial, "this is Pete."

Pete looked as though he might pass out.

"Come on," Julia said, and led him down the hall to the bathroom suite connected to her bedroom. He leaned against the sink and she handed him a wad of toilet paper for his nose. His eyes swam behind his glasses, so she took them off and set them on the counter.

"Hi," he said, over her shoulder. Julia looked into the mirror and saw Gary filling up the doorway behind her.

"Who are *you*?" Gary asked.

Pete extended his free hand and said his name from behind the toilet paper. Gary raised his eyebrows.

"We're going to the movies," Julia said, applying a cool washcloth to Pete's head. "Or maybe the hospital. How's the ribs, Pete?"

"This is some kind of date?" Gary asked. "Were you in a wreck or something?"

Pete shook his head. "Sword fight."

Gary shook his head, laughed too loud. "Fucking sword fight! Perfect! Julia, can I talk to you alone for a minute?"

"It's not a date," Julia said. "Pete's gay."

Pete's forehead crumpled as he lowered the toilet paper.

"Betty told me," Julia said.

"Why?" He looked genuinely confused.

"Because you are?" Gary folded his arms and leaned against the door jamb. "Obviously."

"Shut up, asshole," Julia said to Gary.

Pete wrapped an arm around his ribs and grabbed his glasses. "I'm outta here," he said. "Thanks for the help, Julia." He nodded at Gary, but Gary did not move.

"Pete here thought he had a movie date," Gary said, as Pete pushed past him and made for the hallway.

Julia asked him to wait, but Pete had already stopped beside her desk, where the headless, semi-articulated chimp lay prone. He reached over and flipped on the lamp.

"Well." Pete leaned closer and touched the delicate clavicle. "What in the world is this?" Julia closed her eyes, briefly, white light flashing.

"Got your left and right metatarsals mixed up here, Julia." Pete said from across the room. He paused, and added softly: "Sometimes, I think it was just easier to be a lesbian." He moved a small bone across the desk, clearly calmed by the presence of the chimp.

"You're a girl?" Gary's eyes swept Pete from head to toe. A slow, ironic smile spread across Pete's unshaven face. "Get the fuck out," Gary said, his voice low and even.

"Happy to," Pete answered, but he paused at the doorway, took a step backward, and snapped the fishing wire holding the left leg to the pelvis. "I'll just return this tomorrow," he said. Julia felt the dislocation in her own body, rage like a hot pain all through the tops of her legs. She was grateful for Gary, at that moment, who crossed the room in three long steps and shoved Pete hard against the window frame. Julia didn't move. Pete caught the bottom of Gary's chin with the long yellow femur, and then Julia heard Pete's ribs break, cleanly, against Gary's fist. That pinpoint of light returned; Julia's future self reminding her that she didn't want anything she couldn't stop.

Though unapologetic and still plainly disgusted, Gary was persuaded to drive Pete and Julia to the ER at St. David's, where Pete tumbled out of the back seat and made his way up the drive without looking back.

THE NEXT MORNING, Julia was not surprised to get a call from her supervisor at JoAllen Primates, who told her that the company would not press charges as long as Julia returned the bones.

Julia agreed. "What do you guys do with the skeletons, anyway?"

There was a short silence on the other end of the line. "I liked you, Julia," said her supervisor. "I thought you had a real talent for this kind of work."

Julia hung up the phone and looked at her amalgamation, left leg broken, right arm healed. She went out back to her father's workshop again and found a warped cardboard box. Julia lifted the bones and laid them inside, unable to cut the fishing wire.

When it Happens

For Frank Goldberg

Thursday Night

FRANKIE SWITCHED HER phone to silent and threw it on top of the travel duffel her father had given her for graduation five years before. While she zipped her coat, she paused for a quick look in the mirror hanging over her childhood bed. That's not my face, she thought.

It was Thanksgiving Day. She passed her parents in the den and squeezed her dad's shoulder.

"Going for a walk," she said quietly. He gave her a half smile and returned his attention to a *CSI* rerun.

The cold was dry and windless, the neighborhood as dark as she'd ever seen it. Her childhood streets had been the victim of a series of bad city council decisions, and had been under construction for almost a year. Street lamps were gone, the lanes sheared down to rough red clay and left unpaved, brackish oily runoff collecting in overgrown drainage ditches. Her new boots wouldn't look that way long. Frankie walked slowly down the street where she'd spent her summers skateboarding and playing baseball with her friends in the neighborhood, where they'd dramatically dodged the occasional neighborhood car as though it were an oncoming train. All those boys, now grown, were probably home again tonight, settled in for the evening with light beer and leftover pie. She didn't know any of them anymore.

She'd moved to Madison six months before to work at AIDS Services as a volunteer coordinator. There were seventeen people awaiting assignment the Monday after Thanksgiving, and a big Hanukah event in the works for the second week of December. Frankie planned the community-wide vegan No-Thanks, Giving Potluck and then she'd left a few hours before the party started. She'd told her family that she was only home for a visit, but the truth was that she'd been given a one-way ticket to home to Peaksville in lieu of her last paycheck.

Frankie's older sister Esme called home on Wednesday morning and canceled her family's visit because the baby was puking. Frankie heard the elaborate lie unfolding on the household speakerphone.

"Our house smells like Bigfoot's backside," Esme said. "Bob's starting to feel a little wonky, too. Just a matter of time before we all have it."

Frankie dropped half a banana into a blender full of frozen strawberries and yogurt. She turned it on, but could still hear strains of her mother's soothing response to Esme.

Frankie made it to the bus station just before midnight. She took fifteen dollars out of her wallet and bought the last ride to Lake Burton. There was only one other person on the bus, and he fired two questions about the Mexican takeover at her before she even sat down. She picked a window seat as far away from him as possible, and watched the Peaksville streetlights get farther and farther apart as the bus climbed into the foothills of the Blue Ridge Mountains. She turned her overhead reading lamp off so her reflection in the window wouldn't stare so.

The bus pulled into the station just past midnight. Frankie thanked the bus driver, who replied that young men should be home with their mothers on Thanksgiving. She thought about correcting him, but ended up agreeing instead. If he was just concerned for her safety, better that he thought she was a young man than a fully grown woman. She waited until the bus had moved on before starting up the street in its wake.

It was at least ten degrees colder up there near the lake, but Frankie was still pretty cozy in her parka. She pulled her wool cap out and pushed it down over her short black hair. There was a hollow ache inside her right ear, originating at a long scar over her right temple. The cold had a way of re-invigorating it.

She'd been thinking this plan through the past few years, but last holiday, she'd chickened out and gone to get drunk with her sister instead. They'd walked into the Lion's Head, filled with other Thanksgiving escapees, and ordered tequila. The next morning she woke up in her old bedroom, curled against her sister's back like they were kids. Frankie wished she could revisit all 365 mornings since and figure out which moment, exactly, had sealed this fate upon her heart.

It was always going to be like this, she thought. It couldn't be any different. There was no panic in those thoughts. She made her way through the stripped pine brush down by the water and sat down at the foot of a ramshackle old dock. The sky was clear out over the water, the milky way misting across the tops of the pines at the other side of the lake.

Nobody back home or in Madison knew about Lake Burton, her solo treks across Blue Ridge, but it wasn't a big secret or anything. She'd camped many times with friends throughout high school and college, and had even been to this abandoned dock to swim a few times.

She pulled her cap down low over her forehead and waded into the water. The lake came swirling down through the tops of her boots, which were waterproof. She would never want to drown, she thought, as the still surface of the lake erupted into tiny ripples that broke up the moon's reflection. A million moons.

The shivering stopped shortly after she'd found a thick pine and positioned herself at its base. There was only one moon in the sky as she fell asleep, thinking of animals and their winter habits.

Thursday Night

Frankie announced she was going for a walk as she passed her parents in their big recliners. They were watching *CSI* instead of football. A bloody woman, naked save for heels, was twisted into a corner behind some alleyway dumpsters. Two men raised her eyeless head with gloved hands and shared a knowing look. Frankie's dad was already asleep, chin to chest.

The cold was dry and windless, the neighborhood as dark as she'd ever seen it. Her childhood streets had been the victim of a series of bad city council decisions, and had been under construction for almost a year. Street lamps were gone, the lanes sheared down to rough red clay and left unpaved, brackish oily runoff collecting in overgrown drainage ditches. It was a quiet neighborhood, close to the junior high, full of retirees who used to be young parents with kids who ran wild in the alleyways and rocky creek beds with Frankie. She didn't care if she never saw those streets again.

Frankie checked her watch. He would be by any minute.

Her father was dying in the recliner, slowly, of congestive heart failure, having recovered from two major heart attacks and a mild stroke. First his ankles went, and then his heart and brain and now his very presence. He was only half there any time he opened his eyes after a nap. There was a direct two-hour flight from Madison to Atlanta. In a swift compact rental, Frankie could be doorstep to doorstep in four hours. This promise to her mother, and weekly phone calls, kept them in a relationship of sorts.

Frankie pulled her cap down low over her forehead as a dark little Prius pulled silently to the curb. She got in and buckled up as Rick floored it and sped out of the neighborhood.

Though they had several friends in common, Frankie had met Rick about a million times before she started realizing that he was pretty much everywhere she went. "Face blindness," he said in response to her awkward apology at their final introduction. "Oliver Sacks has it. He couldn't pick his own wife out of a police lineup."

"How can you fall in love with someone you don't recognize?" Frankie wondered one day while she and Rick stood in line for pulled pork sandwiches at the bowling alley. It was somebody's birthday.

"I guess I'll know when it happens," Rick replied.

Rick's Prius smelled new. He tossed a backpack into Frankie's lap.

"Keep your strength up," he said, offering her a jelly jar full of homemade kombucha. Frankie declined. Her mother's Thanksgiving dinner was still settling in her stomach, which had become unaccustomed to meat. The long autumn in Madison had thinned her out because there were things to do and people to do them with, and so many of those things involved bikes and boats. She'd wanted to stay there forever.

"It's better Esme's not going to try to make it for dinner," Frankie's mother had whispered to her that morning at breakfast. "They're all just passing around that terrible stomach bug. Not a good idea, given your dad's condition."

Frankie sighed and tried to spear the yolk of an egg that turned out to be over easy. She looked her mother in the eyes and tried to think of a way to make her life easier, if only for the rest of the day.

"I love you, Mom," she said, and dropped a piece of toast over the runny yolk.

Frankie didn't know why her own mother couldn't tell when Esme was lying. She'd raised the world's worst liar. Though she would have preferred to see her sister one last time, Frankie couldn't hold a day off against her. Given their father's condition and her colicky baby at home, Esme had not been thrilled to hear about Frankie's decision to move to Madison in May.

"I'm not doing this all by myself," Esme said on the phone when Frankie had been gone from Peaksville a week.

"Nobody said you had to. I'm adult with a credit card. I can get home with a moment's notice."

"Tell me the truth, Francesca," she continued, lowering her voice, "what are you doing over there? Is it some cult? You can tell me. I don't judge."

"It's not a cult. It's a nonprofit."

"That does not make me feel better."

Frankie said, "You should come visit. Bring the baby. You'll love it here. I've never been happier." She meant it. She missed her nephew, and she wanted to share something good, for once, with her Esme.

"Communes are for hippies. They'll probably try to call the baby Feather or Moonglow or something."

"Two roommates in downtown Madison is hardly a commune."

"I just miss you."

"I know. I'll be back for Thanksgiving."

"Okay, but don't tell Dad about any of this *Frank* business. And for the love of Christ, just let your hair grow a little. You come home with a flat top again and he'll blow his last stent."

RICK HAD OFFERED to take her as far as the state line, and after that, she was going to hitch to a bus station. She'd told him she was going to New York City, though secretly, she'd rather die than fight all those people every day for a scrap of food, a place to live, a shitty job. She pulled her wallet out of her back pocket and replaced her driver's license and social security card with the ones Rick had put in the bag. Frank Baldwin. Nobody would be searching for Frank Baldwin because he was already dead.

I'll be in touch, Frankie told him at the Tennessee visitor's center at 2 a.m. that morning. His face was unworried and maybe even joyful, patinated by the moon tower's light through raindrops just forming on the windshield. He put his hand on her shoulder and drew her close enough to kiss.

"Keep it in a dry, cool place," he said. "It'll last for a year, and then you're on your own."

Frankie opened the backpack and withdrew a handful of individually packaged needles and a large bottle of testosterone cypionate. There were a couple of shirts and a pair of jeans in there, too, and all of her savings in cash. She counted it, then handed Rick his money and a letter he'd promised to deliver to her family in a year's time. She thanked him and got out of the car just as the wind picked up.

Thursday Night

Thanksgiving Day brought the autumn's first real freeze. By eleven that evening, the cold was dry and windless, the neighborhood as dark as she'd ever seen it. A few earnest houses were already wrapped in Christmas lights. Frankie tipped her earphones up over the crown of her cap and pulled the brim down over her eyebrows. She drew a pack of cigarettes out of her inside coat pocket and lit one right in front of the Junior High mascot. She sat for a few minutes on the bench beside the six-foot beaver and watched a couple of mechanical wire reindeer bob their heads in unison on the lawn across the street. It was so quiet she could hear their motors whirring. A chill shot across her shoulder blades; it was either the cold seeping in through the seams in her jacket or the reindeer moving around with no eyes and no heart.

There were few days to consider her options. She'd only been in Madison six months, after all, and she might be able to beg her old job at the Peaksville library back. She could tell everyone she'd moved home to be with her ailing father. It would sound like the right thing to do. If pressed, she could lie and tell people that AIDS Services lost its funding. If pressed, she could lie and tell them there was a bad relationship. If drunk, she might admit that she'd been fired for fucking a client—one she loved, however briefly, but who did not love her back.

At the end of Winter Lotus Road sat a red brick ranch-style that had been empty for more than a decade. The overgrown yard was a favorite place for the neighborhood kids to gather; Frankie still kept handmade maps of the creek that wound around behind the house and toward the river at the edge of town. She and Jeremy Dorsky spent their spring breaks damming tadpoles into a little cove and raising frog armies. They'd built a pine-bough raft using the directions on the back of a *Boy's Life* magazine and set sail for the river. When it fell apart a half a mile down the creek, he'd cried silently on the bank, his eyes full of anger and deep despair. It was before he learned to hide what he wanted.

Once they got to junior high, he'd only sneak off with her on the weekends when there was nothing better to do. Frankie didn't mind so much until he started telling everyone at school that they were having sex when all they were doing was building a fort. She confronted him in the courtyard behind the cafeteria and he told her everyone thought she was some kind of lesbian.

"You look like a boy," he said. "People think you're weird."

"I've always looked like this," Frankie said.

"Exactly."

"People never thought I was weird before," she insisted. Jeremy shook his head like she didn't know anything about anything.

"I'm doing you a favor," he insisted. "Trust me." Then he walked off with her virginity.

Frankie was surprised to see the porch lit at the house on Winter Lotus Road. A little blue SUV sat in the driveway; a basketball hoop had been installed over the garage doors. She paused on the sidewalk, feeling a sadness move through her limbs the way pain radiates from an injury the split second before you see what you did to yourself. She wanted to get closer—she'd planned to walk back there in the dark again to see if some of the trails were still visible—but now someone lived there. She saw a shadow move past the curtains in the kitchen window, and then the light was gone.

Frankie waited for a solid ten minutes on the sidewalk. The house was asleep, she was sure, so she made her way into the backyard under the cover of the pines down by the water. Then she crossed at the rock bridge they'd nicknamed Golden Gate and ducked under a fallen trunk. The trail was still there. Frankie pulled her keychain flashlight out of her pocket, cursing herself for leaving her phone back at the house. The trail was still visible, if a little overgrown. She had just started in the direction of the old fort when she heard a noise behind her.

ONE CHILLY SATURDAY in eighth grade, she'd agreed to meet Jeremy for a midnight campfire at the fort. Her parents had to agree because, as she pointedly argued, they'd let her camp out in his backyard only two weekends before. She darted past the empty house on Winter Lotus Road and waited at the trailhead for a while before making her way to the fort on her own. He was bringing the matches and the marshmallows. She'd brought chocolate bars and a few graham crackers stolen from her sister's lunch stash for the week. Plenty of firewood was already stacked in the fire-pit near the fort.

She made it to the fort and switched on the Coleman lamp hanging from the ceiling. It swung in lazy cold circles above the butcher-block table they'd dragged from Jeremy's house. She pulled her jacket tight and flipped through a MAD magazine, wishing she'd brought the matches herself.

"Frankie?"

Frankie froze. It wasn't Jeremy.

"Frankie? You in there?"

"Is Jeremy there?"

Whoever it was laughed. "Uh, no." The door opened and Frankie was relieved to see Dalton, her lab partner from third period biology, behind it. They'd dissected a pig just the week before, and he'd slipped the little pink brain into the lunchbox of an unsuspecting seventh grader during the passing period. He was a riot.

"Hey! How'd you find this place?" she asked.

"Jeremy told me about it."

"Did you bring the marshmallows or something?" She asked.

Dalton smiled confusedly.

"For the s'mores." Frankie pointed to the graham crackers and chocolate on the table.

Dalton leaned against the table and rubbed his hands together. "He didn't say anything about marshmallows."

"You got any matches? Frankie asked.

"I got a light," Dalton said, pulling a pack of cigarettes and a lighter from his pocket. He shook a cigarette out for himself and lit it. "You want one?"

"Just the lighter," Frankie said.

"Maybe after, then," Dalton said.

"After what?" Frankie asked. "It's freaking cold out. I don't want a cigarette. I want a fire."

She pulled kindling from a coffee can under the table and took it out to the fire-pit, where she laid the dry branches, sticks and newspaper the way she'd been taught. It only took a minute or so to get a healthy fire going. She retrieved a couple of pieces of plywood from the side of the fort and threw them down on the ground next to the fire. Dalton watched her from the doorway of the fort, fidgeting with his cigarette.

"Well, come on," Frankie said. "Get warm."

Dalton stepped over the plywood she'd set out for him, and sat down next to Frankie instead. Instinctively, she scooted off the wood and onto the cold ground.

"I still have chocolate," Frankie said, and as she moved to stand up, Dalton grabbed her. His hands were long and cold and clammy on the back of her neck as he pulled her close enough to kiss. His breath was smoky and minty, like he had been chewing gum before he lit the cigarette. She pushed him back and made it to her feet, but he caught up with her at the Golden Gate and tackled her as easy as he would one of the calves at the fair. She landed hard on one shoulder and felt it pop, but she managed to bloody his nose with her good elbow as she struggled to right herself beneath his body. Dalton clutched his nose with one hand and brought a fist-sized rock down hard against her left temple. Frankie's eyes rolled like marbles in a shoebox and she felt her dinner surge into her throat.

"What is the problem?" he asked, breathlessly, straddling her hips. "Why did you run?" Frankie, half blind with pain and rage, landed a punch just below his rib cage. It wasn't as hard as she'd have liked, but Dalton rolled off and lay on his back beside her.

He said he was sorry.

THIS TIME, THE twigs snapping behind her were not frightening. Frankie was no calf. She'd worked herself into the shape of a fire hydrant, her hands strong as hammers. She could deadlift her own weight and she wasn't scared of anyone. Someone stepped into the beam of her little flashlight.

"Hi."

Frankie shined the light directly into the woman's eyes. It was no one she recognized. "I saw you waiting on the street," the woman said.

"I apologize for sneaking around. I get this is creepy."

The woman shielded her eyes with one hand. "It's cold out here."

Frankie dropped the beam. "I'll take off. I was just looking around."

The woman didn't move. "You cold?"

Frankie shrugged. "A little. But I'll walk it off."

"You want some hot chocolate?"

The house had been restored to a full-on late-70s split-level splendor. Frankie followed the woman onto the screened back porch and deposited her shoes and coat next to the door. The golden carpet in the den had tree branch patterns sewn into the shag. Music drifted from another room. The den was all over built-in shelves, floor to ceiling books and music.

"I brought this chocolate from Mexico," the woman said as she handed a mug to Frankie and sat down on the couch. She wore a brilliant red turtle-neck under a tastefully dark cardigan and had the kind of face that telegraphed what her youth had given and what her future would be. Both were beautiful. "I only drink it when it's below freezing outside. That way, I don't go through it too quickly."

Frankie removed her hat and ran her fingers through her short hair. The fresh air feathered around her scalp and ears as she leaned back against the arm of the couch. "I always thought this place was empty," she said, eyeing the books. It would take forever to get through them all.

"It looked that way for a long time," the woman admitted. "I remember you, I think. You were always dragging something interesting down to the creek. There was a pretty impressive fort at one time, if I remember correctly."

"Did you find the stash of Pall Malls?" Frankie asked.

"I didn't think you'd come back."

"I didn't plan to," Frankie said, wondering if the woman had been there the night Jeremy forgot to bring the marshmallows. She looked from the woman's mug of chocolate to her own strange reflection in the back bay window that opened up to the pine stand down by the creek. *That's not my face*, she thought.

"You say you've been here a while?"

"You didn't know?"

Beyond the pane of glass, it was so quiet and lovely, bare branches dark against a lightening sky. Frankie closed her eyes just briefly, thinking of the winter habits of all the waiting animals.

Abuses of History

Above Bunny's ancient Toyota, great black flocks of grackles are on the move. They edge the telephone lines along the highway, migrating from one small town parking lot to another. Two hours from home, Bunny pulls off IH35 and into an Exxon station. While the numbers are running on the gas pump, she walks inside the store to use the restroom and looks at the skin on her neck. The washroom smells of antiseptic and menstrual blood. One of the corners of the mirror above the sink has cleaved, revealing the opaque green backing of the glass, and there is a long crack running from one side to the other. The hives on her neck are creeping down her shirt.

She buys a pack of cigarettes and a grape Nehi soda at the counter and turns to see a man outside bending over the front bumper of her car.

"Hey," she shouts from across the parking lot. The man straightens, and she can see he's got a pocketknife in his hand, blade extended. In one fluid movement, he folds the blade back and slides the little plastic sheath into the pocket of his jeans. He's a little older than her, maybe thirty, but he seems friendly. She steps between the pumps and looks down at the grille.

"You hit a bird," he says, pointing at the fluttering feathers, flat streaks of wind-dried blood painting the bottom of her fiberglass bumper.

"Just trying to get it off," he continues, bending to pick up the bottle, which has rolled from her feet to his.

Bunny fights a wave of nausea. She turns her back, ashamed he could guess she would not be able to stomach the sight of blood and beak. The man hands her the soda, which, she thinks numbly, is now probably flat.

It has been ages since she's traveled the roads from Rockport to La Grange, and she finds the landscape has sweetened, somehow, in the intervening years. She hasn't been home since her father's funeral a few years back. She's missed the trip—fields growing grayer against the horizon line, slow horses searching for winter grass beneath mesquites.

She fumbles the cap to the Nehi and a fountain of carbonation ends up in her lap. Bunny half-searches through a stack of CDs for one that doesn't make her sick, and tries not to think of her mother until she has to.

WHEN SHE ARRIVES at the farmhouse, Bunny tries three different keys on the ring before she finds the one that works the deadbolt. The first floor of the farmhouse is dark and quiet and smells of cedar oil. Bunny figures her mother and aunt to be asleep upstairs. She opens the door to her old bedroom to find that her mother has transformed the room into a pink-and-white festival of satin and chiffon. There's a china doll sitting against the bed pillows. No trace of Bunny remains: her decrepit garage sale desk is gone, as are the horse posters and collection of twisted sticks from the creek. She knows she shouldn't expect things to be the same, but the bedroom feels incriminating. There's not a trace left of the girl she once was. Bunny kicks her bag out into the hallway and shuts the bedroom door, thinking she'd rather sleep on the couch than in that bed.

The toilet flushes, and Bunny's Aunt Sophie appears down the hallway, drying her hands on her thighs. Her smile is wide and strong, like the rest of her body, and she folds Bunny into a hug redolent of Merle Norman. "Didn't even hear you come in!"

"I missed you," Bunny mumbles into Sophie's shoulder. Bunny doesn't try to disentangle herself from her aunt. In truth, it feels good to be pinned by someone stronger than herself. Sophie, her mother's twin, was made sturdy and peaceful by their small-town childhood, and had spent her life teaching parenting classes to pregnant teenagers all over Texas. She'd been a solid holiday touchstone, and the only phone call Bunny could make when she fell in love with her high school softball teammate Janelle.

"We've missed you, too," she says, "though the place is a lot easier to keep up since the sale."

Shortly after her father's death, Bunny's mother sold the family's seventy-five acres of land—two fields flanked by a fat, healthy creek and a looming, two-hundred-foot limestone outcrop—to a neighbor who promptly opened the Rockin' J Dude Ranch and began building state-of-the-art cabins in the back field. Bunny's mother still lives in the farmhouse—she had it written into the contract that her rent on the house be frozen until the day of her death.

Upstairs in the guest bedroom, Bunny's mom is sleeping. "You know she had them carry her up here after the surgery. Said it gets better light," Sophie explains. She points to the emergency numbers on the bedside table and tells Bunny that a home health nurse comes twice a day.

"This is probably a mistake," says Bunny. Sophie turns around. Bunny can see there is little patience left in her eyes.

"A long overdue mistake, then."

Bunny looks at her mother, who is slack-jawed and snoring. There is her body, under a flat sheet, bare save for the thick white bandage holding together the bisected belly underneath. "I won't know what to do," Bunny says, afraid to be alone with such a body.

Sophie lifts the suitcase easily, her thick freckled forearms visible under a white muslin top. "You'll be fine. She'll be fine. I'm only gone until Wednesday."

Her mother lifts her head and shifts her weight stiffly, eyes still closed. Bunny fights an urge to touch the clean white sheet, to run her fingers up the exposed arm and feel for a heartbeat at the side of her mother's neck. Instead, she takes a deep breath and announces to the sleeping woman that she will return after she unpacks.

SHE DECIDES TO stay in the master bedroom. Back when the room belonged to both her mom and dad, Bunny liked to sneak into their closet and sit among the shoes strewn at the bottom. She'd close herself in and peer through the slats in the doors, waiting for an opportunity to spring at the calves of an unsuspecting parent. Now, from the other side of the room, the closet feels haunted. She has to pry her eyes from the door, and convince herself that nobody's watching her from the other side. She sits down at the little desk under the window. Outside, the same familiar fields roll toward the creek.

On the table next to the phone is a yellowing rolodex. The first few cards in the rolodex contain lists of names written in her father's handwriting–business contacts and hunters who spent more time on his land than their own. She flips through the family friends, her aunts, uncles, and finally comes to the card with her own name at the top. The last address showing is one she left three years ago.

Bunny lifts a thick fountain pen from its brassy executive holder, crosses out the old address, and writes down her new information. She flips the cards back to the front, and then calls her girlfriend.

"I made it," she says when Gina picks up.

"Frankie's brought pizza," Gina says, happily. "And *Braveheart*." Bunny hears somebody popping the top on a beer.

"Is the dog in there?" she asks.

"Frankie, she's calling you a dog." Gina's voice is loud and thin over the line.

Frankie takes the phone and tells her he's brought her fourteen small jobs for next week. Bunny repairs antique jewelry and Frankie owns a consignment store, and they do their best to keep one another in business.

"I just cleaned the couch," Bunny explains. "You keep Luna on the floor, okay?"

"Sure, yeah," Frankie says. Bunny hears the dog hit the hardwoods of her living room.

"I gotta go," she says. "I miss you guys."

"Don't let the country air ruin your lungs," Frankie says. "Busy week next week. Here's Gina."

"I love you," she says to Gina.

"How bad is it?" Gina asks. Bunny can tell by the slight echo that she's shut herself into the bathroom for privacy. "Don't lie."

"It's not that bad."

Gina lets the line go quiet for a moment. "I love you, too," she says.

In her mother's room, Bunny searches for a power cord, plugs in her phone, and then feels around the side pocket of the recliner. There's an old Rosamunde Pilcher paperback in there, along with the TV remote. Behind Bunny, there is a cough, and she turns to see her mother's eyelids flutter. An instant of wild panic flashes across her mother's face. A few minutes later, her mother blinks groggily and turns her head. "You're hiving" she says.

"How do you feel?" Bunny asks, pouring water into an adult sippy-cup from the hospital.

"Like major organs are missing."

"Sophie said your nurse'll be here pretty soon." Bunny lowers the straw to her mother's lips and smells the blue-black odor of dulled pain.

"I had Sophie call you when I went in for surgery. I only had a few hours to put things in order."

"How could you not know?" Bunny asks as she hears the door open downstairs.

"It started small, like everything," her mother replies. "You want me to call you every time I'm gassy?"

A short slim woman with large hands strides into the room. "Well!" she says brightly. "You must be Bunny!"

"I'll leave it to you, then," Bunny says. "I'll be downstairs."

On the stairs, she hears the nurse opening her bag and saying, "You know, she doesn't look like a Bunny."

"She never did," says her mother.

BUNNY DECIDES TO survey the damage herself, get it over with. She walks past the abandoned goat pen in the back field and down a worn animal trail to the creek, thinking that the Rockin' J Dude Ranch idea, while stupid, will probably turn out to be more lucrative than anything her father ever came up with. He didn't grow up in the country, around animals in fields. He'd been an Army brat, and had lived in five countries by the time he married Bunny's mother at twenty.

"I thought he was a man of the world," she'd told Bunny over and over, in response to any question regarding the land, the struggling farm. "Handsome, funny, spoke Japanese and gave me a German fairy tale book on our second date." Her mother, unlike Sophie, had despised their small coastal hometown, and believed the gifts of foreign language to be promising signs of travel and wealth. When her husband bought the seventy-five acres a few miles outside of LaGrange and began slowly renovating the farmhouse, she almost divorced him. She left, at least. She got as far as Salt Lake City in a VW bus she'd bought cheap off a dealer in La Grange.

"But by then I was five months gone and showing. He flew up and got me, and I never even got to Idaho." That's where the story ended. She was nineteen.

A man of the world her father was not. When he traveled, it was to pick up feed or bring home new stock. He bred goats, then quarter horses, then Dexter cattle. There were always a couple of tiny bulls grazing in the back field and a feeble corn crop dying of thirst in the front. Eventually, in response to a poaching problem, her father began leasing the land to a steady stream of hunters who set up themselves up in the woods around the bottom of the limestone mountain, spreading deer corn and bottled doe urine in wide circles around their badly camouflaged blinds. They were big, rangy men who spent the colder nights in the bottom bedrooms of the farmhouse, joining the family for three square meals a day and evenings of cards and dominoes.

His father's Army friend Miguel would come down from Fort Polk to spend his vacation weeks hunting and fishing on the land, turning his catch into gumbo or jambalaya. Her mother seemed to welcome the distraction from the tedium, and during the colder months, Bunny often went to sleep with the sounds of their drunken stories drifting up through the wooden floorboards. There was always a lovely crawfish stew on the stove those nights, or a roast in the oven.

Bunny hunts around in the weeds by the creek for a bit and finds the trace of an old path. She follows it up along a ridge overlooking the water, and finally comes to a small area covered over in broken mesquite branches and sourspot bushes. Hidden from the farmhouse, she sits down and pulls her knees to her chest. A hazy February sun is beginning to set behind the bare black limbs on the other side of the creek. She wasn't given to fancy as a child, but there were some things both undeniable and untenable. This land knows her name, and soon she will be lost to it.

Back down by the house, Bunny swings the barn doors open and is surprised to find her father's ancient John Deere with a shiny new baler attached to the rear. The rest of the barn is empty, save for a few piles of lumber. She pushes the other door open to let in more light and walks to the corner stall, where her father kept the baby goats who weren't going to make it on their own. She inhales, hoping for a trace of animal. All she gets is motor oil.

There was a time when she tried to save a kid on her own, in the fall of her thirteenth year. He'd been left by the rest, unable to stand, heart beating too hard against the shell of his narrow chest. He was little bigger than a puppy, his front legs misshapen. Sweating beneath the warmth of his body, she carried him to the barn, speaking quietly, reassuringly, in the manner of her father.

She'd set him down in the brittle hay of the back stall, and started looking for a bottle. When she couldn't find the red and yellow nipple immediately, a slow panic began to spread through her chest. She lifted reedy blankets and turned over dusty equipment in the falling light, her hands trembling and raw with cold. Every few minutes she returned to the kid to feel his chest, check his beleaguered breathing. Red foam bubbled at his lips. After a while, frantic and shaking, she knelt beside him, pushed handfuls of hay against his body to keep him warm, and ran for the house.

"I've got a kid in the barn," she announced in the kitchen. Her mother stood at the sink, pouring red wine into a coffee mug. Dan, a red-headed hunter who practically lived with them during deer season, looked up from his bowl of chili and continued speaking as if nothing had happened. Bunny's mother sat down across from him and lifted the wine to her lips. "I need the bottle," Bunny said, raising her voice over Dan's. "That one with the red and yellow nipple. Do you know where Dad put it?"

"Are you serious?" Her mother never went near the barn.

"He's going to die if he doesn't eat," Bunny said.

"Gonna die anyway," Dan said quietly, sopping chili grease with a piece of buttered bread.

Bunny shook her head, now frustrated more than panicked, and got halfway up the stairs before she heard her mother say, "He's not up there. He'n Miguel drove to Houston to see about that Alpaca herd." Dan said something to her mother in a low voice, and Bunny left through the back door to avoid passing them again.

"Hunting season's OVER!" she yelled at the house from a safe distance. "GO HOME!"

She returned to the barn, wishing her father knew the way Dan acted when he wasn't around. Like he owned the place, her mother, her self.

In the barn, she flipped on the inside light, took a deep breath, and made herself concentrate on the colors she needed: Red. Yellow. Red. Yellow. She forced her eyes to bring each object into focus. Her heart slowed. It was just one thing. One thing she could not find.

Bunny walked back to the kid, who was on his side, stiff legged. Red-threaded mucus pooled in the hay beneath his cheek. She knelt, pushed more hay against his belly and sat back on her heels. Behind her, the kitchen screen door slammed. Her mother called. She shut the barn doors, knowing the kid would die sometime during the night.

THE NEXT MORNING Bunny is awakened by the thin, terrible sound of the mower. She unfolds herself from the easy chair beside her mother's bed and stretches. A green John Deere cuts a line across the pasture she walked every morning before school. Bunny has coffee ready by the time the nurse arrives. She brings a breakfast tray and stays to watch Trudy tend to her mother.

"It doesn't even hurt today," says her mother in a surprised tone, watching the nurse swab. Her wound has been left open, to drain and heal on its own.

Bunny keeps her eyes on the tray until her mother gasps at a sore spot. Then Bunny looks, and there are layers. Parts of her mother that exist beneath the skin, parts that are not meant to see light.

By the time the bandage is pulled tight again, the coffee is cold. Bunny sits and listens to the easy conversation between her mother and the nurse, watches her mother swallow pills and attempt to readjust herself on the pillows. After the nurse leaves, her mother looks flushed and tired, but alert.

"Give me some of that coffee," she says. "It's been ages."

Bunny fills a cup. "It's cold."

"So it takes stage three to get you back home," says her mother.

"It takes stage three to get an invitation."

"You're letting your hair grow?"

"Nah, just laziness."

"Your dad always liked it longer."

Bunny touches the back of her neck. She wants to say that she thought of him the first time she could pull her hair into a ponytail again. That sometimes she wakes up in the morning, having forgotten he is gone. And that she doesn't want to feel so lost and angry about the farm, but she can't begin to imagine a line of strangers trail riding along the creek bed. Her mother nods at the ring on Bunny's finger.

"How's Gina?

"Not crazy about moving to Rockport, but I got a good deal going with Frankie. Gina's boss is willing to let her work from home, so we're gonna try it for a while."

"I have trouble believing you're going to be there long. Nobody moves there on purpose."

"Your parents did. Besides, no jobs but the big boxes in the city," Bunny says. "It was soul-crushing." She also wants to be as far as possible from anything resembling the farm.

"Is she coming to visit while you're here?"

"Here? Mom, there's a *Welcome Cowboys* sign in our driveway. There's a ropes course in our back field."

"This is still our house."

"It's the Rockin'J Mess Hall," Bunny says. "They're just waiting until you kick off before they install a buffet."

Her mother's face goes hard. "Your daddy didn't leave me much choice in the matter, Bunny. Remember that."

Bunny takes the coffee from her mother's hands and puts it back on the tray.

"Caffeine's not good for healing."

When Bunny returns from the kitchen, her mother is dozing in front of a muted episode of *Oprah*. Bunny sits, opens her book, and watches Oprah give away dreams.

Close to dinner time, Bunny grills a hamburger patty, melts cheese over it, and places a crisp, cold tomato on top. She adds a little pepper and salt, then takes the plate upstairs.

Her mother smiles when she sees the meal, one of her old favorites, and goes a little soft around the corners of her mouth.

"You want to try to come to the table? Trudy says you need to try to move around every couple of hours."

"I'm tired."

Bunny spent her childhood in silent disagreement with her mother, knowing it was useless to argue. "How about you just try sitting up to eat the burger and you make a decision from there?"

Her mother opens her mouth to disagree, but instead holds up a finger to Bunny's face. "I see what you did there. Very crafty."

Bunny helps her mother into a sitting position, and then offers an arm as support while she pulls her legs over the side of the bed. Her breath comes quick while her limbs move slowly, and the color has gone from her face.

"Take a break," Bunny says.

"Now I'm up I might as well try for the table."

"Three steps, tops," Bunny says, surprised at how light her mother has become, how brittle her shoulders are.

"The bathroom also counts, you know," says her mother, using her arms to lower herself gingerly into the wooden seat. "Trudy says I'm supposed to be moving around every couple hours. Ha. Trudy's so full of shit. Never been sick a day in her life. You remember her? Used to be your nurse in elementary school long time ago."

"No," Bunny says.

Her mother takes a small bite of tomato. "I know you're mad at me."

"I'm fine."

"You are, or you'd have been back to see me."

"I'm really fine."

"You want me to apologize? I can do that."

"Apologize for what?" Bunny asks. "For Dan?"

Bunny's mother swallows and reaches for the iced tea. She takes a long drink, then sets the tea down and meets Bunny's eyes with curiosity. "Now that's something new. Why would I apologize about Daniel Sinclair?"

"Is there something else you want to apologize for? Sincerely?"

"God, *nothing* sincerely. But you need something from me. It's why you've returned on my deathbed, right?" Her mother leans forward, a mawkish smile spreading across her face. "To wrest from me the secrets of an ill-timed marriage, a mistaken pregnancy, a wasted life?"

Instead of answering, Bunny pretends to respond to a text message.

THE NEXT MORNING brings a short, violent storm across the north side of the farm, stilling construction on the little cabins. Bunny sips coffee while Trudy changes her mother's bandages in the next room, watching the rain sweep across the fields. The creek will be full after the rain clears off, and she makes a mental note to see if any of her father's fishing gear is still in the garage. Three days left, and she and her mother are at a standstill. Her mother answered no questions the rest of the evening prior, so Bunny gave up and went to bed early.

Her idea is not fully formed before she has dialed the number in the rolodex. Electrical impulses traveling down a wire, just as unfathomable as cell towers pinging in the distance. There is only the memory of the back of Dan's head, hair cut so short that white scars were visible on the rolls of fat where his neck met his skull. The smell of gun oil and newspaper spread across the kitchen table.

Bunny is surprised when he answers the phone, and even more surprised to find herself asking Dan if he wants to visit her dying mother. After all these years, she says. Yes.

"WELL," SAYS DAN, offering his hand to Bunny at the door, "Been awhile, hadn't it?" He's jowly and thick, the tips of his black ropers unscuffed.

"You haven't changed much," says Bunny, finding it difficult to return his smile.

"How's she doin'?"

Bunny steps aside to let him in the house. "Coffee?"

"Everything's the same," Dan says, surveying the kitchen and seating himself at the table. "She upstairs?"

"You hear she sold the place?"

Dan shakes his head. "Yeah, terrible. Happens, though. Couple years back, hadda just about do the same myself."

"*You* have land?" Bunny slides a cup of black coffee in front of him but doesn't offer cream or sugar. She knows his place. There's a rotting grain elevator standing on it.

"Hundred acres."

"No deer on your land?"

"Crawling, why?"

"Well, you hunted *this* land. Not your own."

Dan shrugs, looking confused. "Family land gets old. I've hunted all over Texas, Oklahoma, Florida even. Besides that, your mom and dad liked company. Think your mom got lonely out here just the three of you. And God knows they needed the money. And the meat. You taking good care of your mama? You here for long?"

He has the distracted air of men who are not accustomed to being alone with women who aren't possible conquests.

"You never got bored on this land? I remember you being around *a lot.*"

"Don't guess so." Dan sets his cup down and wipes his upper lip with the back of an index finger.

"My mother, she still talks about that time you brought home a baby bobcat."

"Bobcat? I never found one a those I didn't kill."

Bunny stands to retrieve a package of Oreos from the freezer, where her mother has always kept them. Eat them just like candy, she'd say, whatever that was supposed to mean.

"That must have been another one of her hunters," Bunny says. "There were a lot of you."

Dan waves the plate of cookies away. "What's this about?" he asks, not quite looking up.

Bunny shrugs and studies his face, which is clean-shaven, but only just lately. The skin below his nose is white and tender. His eyes narrow. "What kinda joke is this?" he asks. "Your mama is up there, dying looks like, and you got a bone to pick with *me*?" Dan shakes his head, his cheeks flushed. "I swear to God." Dan stands and starts for the stairs.

Bunny slides by him and asks him to stop at the top of the stairs. "Let me tell her you're here," she says. He looks disgusted with her, and pushes past to knock gently on her mother's door.

"She's asleep," Bunny whispers as he turns the knob. Panic rises in her throat and she wants to call out, to warn her mother that she's done something possibly unforgivable. Bunny's mother is not asleep. She's reading. When she looks up, her eyes are large and watery behind the magnifying half-glasses. She is surprised, unfocused, until she sees Dan in the doorway.

"Hi, Dolly," says Dan, his voice soft and melodic with memory or emotion or something else that Bunny can't name. Her mother looks from Dan to Bunny, her expression a lot like the one belonging to the man who scraped the dead bird from Bunny's grille.

"Your Bunny was kind enough to call, said you was feelin' a little under the weather." Dan is still standing in the door, and her mother looks quickly around the room. She sets her jaw, smiles stiffly. She folds her glasses and waves Dan inside.

"Maybe it's not a good time," Bunny says. Her mother acts as though she doesn't hear. She pats the bed and Dan sits.

"You old bastard," she says, not unkindly.

Bunny shuts the door and sits down on the top stair. She puts her head in her hands.

Dan's truck keys sit next to his half-empty coffee cup on the kitchen table downstairs. Bunny grabs them and heads outside to the truck, which is parked between the house and the barn. She doesn't have a plan. She walks around the truck and opens the driver's side door. There's a pouch of Red Man chew wedged between the console and the passenger's seat, and a small bowie knife snapped in a leather boot holster. Bunny pulls the knife from its sheath and runs her finger along the back of the blade. She thinks about slashing Dan's tires, but realizes he'll be stuck on the farm. She decides instead to nail his tires so there'll be a long, slow leak, not necessarily traceable. She settles on that idea, and moving to get out of the cab, she drops the knife. Reflexively, she moves to catch it before it hits the seat, and the tip of the blade catches the soft webbing of skin between her right thumb and index finger.

Bunny grabs her right hand with her left. There's a moment, just before the first drop of blood spatters on the seat, in which Bunny senses a new kind of regret she will feel for the rest of her life. It will still be there after the death of her mother, after the razing of the farmhouse, after the first twenty-year-old brain-dead pack horse is led down the field and onto the creek trail. She will get older, stronger, and further from the truth of who her parents were behind the doors of the farmhouse, beyond her reach. She'll forget her father's face. She'll forgive the sale of the land. But she won't come to live past or without the loss that is just beginning to pull at her back molars. Despite the heady nausea that comes in waves, Bunny sits a full minute in the cab of the truck, watching the blood run down her forearm and onto the seat.

Half an hour later, Dan comes downstairs. Bunny is bandaged and sitting at the table, waiting. Dan pauses at the table and asks what happened to her hand.

"Go away," Bunny says.

When he tries to get back inside, he starts with a concerned knock, which escalates quickly. Dan pounds on the door, then moves to the

French casements over the kitchen sink. He will call the police and come back with his gun get ready for a phone call from his lawyers if Bunny doesn't get out there right this minute and clean up all that blood.

When he leaves for good, Bunny fills a tumbler with bourbon and takes it out onto the porch to watch clouds threading the sky above the house, moving fast to make way for thunderheads coming down from Dallas. The whiskey takes the edge off the pain in her palm, where there's now a new line right down the middle of the heart, head and life lines.

AN HOUR LATER, Bunny's phone rings. "Well, I'm not coming down there," says her mother. "You will have to come up."

Bunny sits at the foot of the bed and asks her mother if she has made things worse by coming to see her.

Her mother ignores the question and asks Bunny if she remembers the time her father took them to the airport to watch the soldiers come home from the Persian Gulf.

"Can we even call people Persian anymore?" her mother asks. "I can never keep up."

"I think they just call it the Gulf War."

Miguel was coming home from a yearlong tour, and Bunny's father meant to meet him at the gate with a bottle of Wild Turkey and pack of Marlboros. He'd never spoken of family and she'd never thought of them until this moment.

"You wore heels," Bunny says.

"Miguel was a sweet man, like your dad."

Bunny remembers the pristine floors and the smell of hot pretzels by the gate. She'd never been on a plane. At first, it was thrilling to see the soldiers all in the same boots, same hats, same bags upon their shoulders. Their sunglasses—how alike did they have to be? It was like a parade.

But once they fell out of step and into the arms of their families, their faces began changing, melting into hollow-eyed replicas of humanity. Bunny had been confused, and then horrified. Miguel, one of the last ones off the plane, rushed into the arms of her father and buried his face deep in his neck. Spared of the shift in Miguel's features, Bunny looked gratefully at her mother, who bore the look of a dental patient trying to make it through a lengthy but necessary root canal.

"He always wanted me along," Bunny's mother says. "And you, too. It wasn't like he didn't love us."

"Where is he now?"

"It was the late eighties. He died the way those young men usually died then. Your father was hurt, but I was just glad he wasn't sick, too."

Bunny takes a deep breath. Before she says anything, her mother holds up one hand.

"Your father and I never had to apologize to each other," her mother says. "I shouldn't have to apologize to you."

When Sophie returns to the house the next morning, Bunny is in the kitchen, sweeping.

Sophie blows on her cupped hands. "It's hot in this house. But it looks like you brought the rain."

"She told me she was cold, so I turned up the heat. You want some breakfast? She didn't eat much."

"Coffee would be nice," Sophie says, bumping the thermostat down and taking a seat at the parquet table. She swipes a few cookie crumbs into her palm and empties them onto the pile that Bunny has swept up. "I see you are both still alive," she says.

"Did you know Miguel?" Bunny asks, measuring the coffee.

"Sure, I knew Miguel," Sophie says, lugging her sack of a purse to the table. She fishes around inside until she finds a pack of Dorals. Bunny casts an anxious look at the ceiling, but her aunt waves it off.

"Stage three," Sophie says. "Hell, *she* can smoke if she wants to."

Bunny helps herself to a cigarette and lights it off the end of her aunt's. "I called Dan Sinclair," she says. "He came to the house."

A short laugh escapes Sophie's throat and turns into a cough. "Oh God, you're playing to win this one. I wish I could've seen the look on your mother's face!"

"They were miserable here, both of them. All of them."

"Oh honey, they made their lives what they could. We all do. I hated that old asshole, Dan, though. I was glad when she was through with him. Used to get drunk and scream and cry and try to shoot out the stars. Scared the horses to bits."

"She won't tell me anything," Bunny says.

"Really. Seems like you've got *some* new information under your belt these past few days."

"I made her mad, that's why. How could you have kept all of this from me?"

"You were a kid." Sophie shrugs like Bunny would have done the same thing. "Now you're an adult." She exhales and points her cigarette at her niece. "Bunny, you need to go up there and tell her you're gonna be okay. Lie if you have to. It's a family virtue."

Bunny does go upstairs, but she doesn't wake her mother. Instead, she packs quietly in the master bedroom before creeping into her mother's room. She pulls a clean sheet from the linen closet, unfurls it over her sleeping mother, and tucks it in at the foot of the bed. Then, she folds the note and tents it over the TV remote on the bedside table; her mother will reach for it after she finds her glasses.

Downstairs, Bunny hugs her aunt at the door and thanks her. She tells Sophie she will be back the next weekend. It took her three tries, but when the words finally came, they felt pulled from a place as hopeful and green as the field where she'd found the abandoned kid.

From Around Here

THE SECOND TIME Cody Sherman put himself in the hospital, I'd been back home in Talcum for less than a month and hadn't even unpacked all the boxes in my little studio. I recognized Cody's senior picture in the paper immediately: lost black eyes over a wide, girlish mouth. The cops found no handwritten manifestos in the pool-house behind his parents' B&B, no secret stashes of coke, no dark evidence of his troubled adolescence—only a couple of five-year-old game consoles and a long red shelf of video-game novelizations. I'd given him all my hot wheels in high school and wondered if one or two were still in that little pool-house apartment.

I'm not proud that I started haunting the hospital while he lay inside, fighting to come up out of a coma. Anybody with any guts would just go inside and say hello to the family. Brush off transition, focus on Cody. Offer to pick up dinner or bring a six-pack by the house. But I didn't. Any time I finished something necessary like class or work, I'd drive to the parking lot of the hospital of the Sherman House and then to Le Chateau Blanc, my own crappy apartment building. Each time I drove this circuit, the heartbeat in my tonsils made them ache.

Drawn to the tragedy because of the quiet boy I'd known, the closest I'd ever come to having a little brother, I fooled myself for a while. But it was Jill Sherman, Cody's sister, who had been my first real infatuation, my first disaster of a relationship. Though I hadn't seen her around, I knew she'd be wandering around her old bedroom upstairs and making vats of coffee for the guests and driving her mother to the hospital every day.

A few days after I started stalking, I noticed little objects appearing on the doorstep of Sherman House. Among the multitude of flowers on his makeshift altar were stuffed animals and candles and pictures. Cards were everywhere, tucked into the door jamb and propped up on the window sill. The Shermans didn't seem to be worrying themselves with bringing anything inside.

One empty, dank afternoon after class, I parked in the empty visitors' lot of Sherman House and walked around back to the courtyard, swallowing past the ache in my throat. Through the blinds in the renovated pool-house, I could see they'd left Cody's stained futon pulled two feet from the screen of his gigantic television set.

"Can I help you?" I turned to see a long-waisted hostess coming across the courtyard, her heels sinking into the mulch as she picked her way through the garden.

"Yes," I said, straightening. "I'm here to inquire about weekday rates?"

She cocked her head at me. "You from around here?" she asked. Nobody in town had yet placed me, but I had grown to favor my mother in a way that earned me a lot of second glances in the grocery store. The hostess was probably just a few years behind me in high school, maybe a cheerleader, given the tautness of her calves.

"Oh, I grew up here," I said, casually as possible. "I have friends visiting in a few weeks, though. I like to keep my business local."

"Is that right," she said. She offered her hand, stiffly. "I'm Tiffany."

I pointed up at the window that used to be part of Jill's closet—a darkened, stained glass tulip framed in teak. "Is that room available?" I asked.

"Isn't that pretty?" Tiffany said, wobbling back over to the sturdier gravel path that led around front. "But I'm afraid that's family living quarters. There's been a family crisis, so the daughter is home, helping her parents for a while. If you'll follow me, I'll get you a copy of the rates. Weekdays, did you say?"

I followed her down the path to the front of the house. It hadn't changed much over five years, save for a few satellite dishes and a couple of new gutters. She let the door go behind her, so I waved her off through the window, pretending my phone was ringing. As I turned to talk to nobody, I plucked a bright red envelope from the top of the stack and made my way back to my car. I drove the circuit once more, this time certain of Jill's presence. This time, sure she could also feel mine.

Back inside my own apartment, I propped the unopened envelope against the linoleum backsplash and washed the dishes. I waited. I cleaned everything—the floors, the tiny bathroom, the top of the fridge. Afterward, I showered and sat down at my desk. I like the smell of cleaning chemicals. Fake pine, bitter lemon. I slid my letter opener under the front flap.

The message was written in a neat, unassuming handwriting.

Dear Cody,
Sometimes I pretend you're still around and I drive down the alley just to see if your light is on. I keep dreaming I'm under you when you fire the gun, and the bullet gets lodged in my throat. I suffocate to death instead of bleed to death, but it's your bullet that does it. I wake up and I'm all sweaty and hot and at first I don't know if I'm soaking in your blood or what.

I put the card into the top drawer of my desk and opened my sociology textbook, but the words inside were unconvincing.

THE BEGINNING OF my junior year of high school, Jill's family moved into a once-resplendent purple Victorian in the middle of town. They remodeled it into a bed and breakfast, named it Sherman House, and began hosting tasteful block parties. Talcum is not a destination, and is too far off the highway to be an unintentional stop along the way to someplace better. It's dying, mostly already dead. The streets are curbed only on the white side of town, but all the good restaurants are on the other side. The college there is third rate, at best, and the students never stick around on the weekends. Jobs in Talcum are for teachers and van drivers and Shell station owners, and nothing at all happens at night, unless you count the teenage keg parties in the cotton fields off the back roads.

But the rooms at Sherman House filled up, somehow, every weekend. Roses bloomed against the yellow trim in the front yard, and live music could be heard from the street on Friday evenings. During the week, retired women's charity groups in town took over: Betas, Catholic Daughters, Baptist Women's Choir. They organized fundraisers, patched quilts, screened anti-abortion documentaries. I tagged along to my mother's Catholic Daughters meeting one Sunday afternoon and found Jill sitting sullenly at the back of the trestled courtyard, smoking. She was my age, and with a handsome brow over steady, light eyes; silver bangles up her left arm, silver earrings down her right ear. I recognized her from the Physical Science wing at school, where I passed her locker every day just before lunch.

"You here for the meeting?" she asked.

"No." I said, "not really." I sat down at a little tin table and wished I had something to do with my hands. "I'm Emily."

"I know."

"My mom says y'all just moved here from Boston."

Jill grunted. I couldn't tell if it was admission or denial. "I see you sometimes," she said, "at school. Don't you have any friends?"

"Sure," I said. "I'm on the newspaper." Jill offered me a cigarette, but I'd never had one. I declined, immediately regretful when I saw her pocket her lighter and ground her butt into a gravel paver. "This pisses my parents off," she said, showing me the butt. "But moving here pissed me off, so."

I told her my dad had been gone for five years, so I didn't feel like I could afford to piss my mom off. She didn't apologize for my dad's absence, the way so many people did. Instead, she stood and waved me over, throwing the cigarette butt into a potted geranium. "There's a stained glass window in my closet. You want to see it?"

I followed her up the stairs to her private entrance, through a parlor, and into her wrecked bedroom. There was money in the overstuffed furniture and soft pecan floors; money in Jill's closet, which glowed golden and red beneath the flowering glass. She opened the door and told me it once was a water closet. Inside, the smoke from her jacket and the nearness of her body made me light-headed. It was possible to hear the women in their heels, distant and muffled by all the winter clothes that Jill would never need in Texas.

Jill and I weren't in any of the same classes at school, but we kept each other company in the physics classroom during lunchtime, where Mrs. Marshall didn't mind our presence as long as we let her grade in peace. I ate my vending machine lunch and did whatever homework I'd left for last minute. Jill's chef father packed his kids' lunches. One lunch, a couple of weeks after we met, Jill handed me a paper bag, identical to hers, with a little quiche inside.

"You need more than Twizzlers to get through the day, so I asked for extra this morning."

"I like my Twizzlers," I said, removing the greasy wax paper from the top of the quiche. There was bacon over the top. It smelled delicious. Jill opened the package of Twizzlers and ripped half the waxy red candy away for herself. My mother pressed a few dollars into my hand every Monday, plenty for the cafeteria lunch, but it seemed a shame to spend that money on rubbery enchiladas and wilted iceberg salads. Instead, I was saving for a new watch.

After school, we'd walk back to the B&B and hang out with Cody while her parents swept and cooked for incoming guests. I liked Cody.

Unlike all the other middle school kids in Talcum, who dressed as though they were destined for a lifetime of Future Farmers of America competitions, Cody wore long t-shirts and carefully ripped jeans and carried a big black sketch book. Even in the heat of September, he kept a ski hat pulled over his forehead and ears, covering long blonde hair he refused to cut or wash much. He was mostly silent, a little folded into himself.

When I started coming around he kept his eyes averted like a woodland creature. I could feel him examining me only when I turned away. His focus was mostly on Jill, however; both of us shadowed her through the maze of narrow hallways, up and down the cracked wooden staircases, into the courtyard. The three of us fell into a rhythm that fall: leftovers in the big kitchen after school, homework on the back porch. Cody would pop in his earbuds and get straight to work like we weren't even there, but if one of us left for the bathroom or a snack, he'd watch, unsettled, until we were all in the same room again. Weekends when I stayed over, Cody fell asleep curled into Jill's papa-san chair, Gameboy in hand. We'd have to grab an armpit each, drag him to his room, and sweep the hot wheels and transformers off his comforter before tucking him under it.

One cold evening in late November, we opened our books and settled in to the newly closed-in back porch. From the outside, it matched the rest of the Victorian. Inside, sunset illuminated the vaulted ceiling, French windows, and soft carpet with light that the rest of the B&B's cramped, paneled rooms would never see. While the dusk settled over us, strains of Neil Young rose quietly from Cody's little boom box.

I was unfocused and floaty. Jill seemed bored by her work; Texas's public high school standards were decades behind her Boston parochial, and she was worried that east coast universities would not take Talcum's class selections seriously. While I struggled to find purchase on the second page of a series of never-ending unbalanced equations, she flew through her physics homework and opened the AP workbook for extra credit.

One moment I was okay, and the next I'd find myself distracted by the fair down growing just below her left ear, or her faint hum of concentration, or the tendons at the back of her right hand. I wanted her help with chemistry, but was too embarrassed to ask. She got up to use the bathroom and dropped a hand on my head as she passed. Once my eyes returned to the problems in front of me, something sweet and faintly nauseating released in my stomach and I had a difficult time remembering why school was important.

"I don't feel great," I said. When she looked up at me, the top of my head tingled. Maybe I was getting sick.

"You want to get a drink?" She asked. Cody lowered his head so his nose was an inch from his drawing. I went to the kitchen and opened the refrigerator, and I was overcome by a powerful wave of whole-body sadness. I chose a few cans of soda and took them with me to the back porch.

"You okay?" Jill asked, moving to the floor where Cody was sprawled, belly down, drawing some kind of monster. She grabbed a soda from the table and slipped a sheet of paper over a hardback book.

"Probably PMS," I said, watching the muscles in her long, beautiful neck as she drained half the soda. I closed my chem book, done trying for the night. I tore a sheet of my own from the back of a spiral and joined them on the floor, throwing a big square eraser into the space between them. Jill studied her brother's drawing for a bit, and then began something of her own.

Cody's monster had a tail spiked with nails and an open mouth full of needle teeth. He tiled the monster's body with scales that grew smaller the further they traveled up its body. Jill's paper had four equal sections. In one, she drew a delicate sword. In another, she was working on a nicely rendered firearm that involved a fat flaming arrow. A few locks of hair had loosened from her ponytail, the ends hovering an inch or so from the paper.

"What's his weakness?" Jill asked Cody. He shrugged, pausing to look up at her.

"Fine," Jill said. "Make it hard, then."

I drew the only thing I could, a cartoon rabbit with a carrot in its mouth, before I pointed at the sword at the top of Jill's page. "That's pretty nice."

"Thanks," she said, holding the paper so I could see properly. "Which one of these sick weapons could kill that monster Cody's working on?" Cody froze. Jill held my eyes for so long that I tasted metal at the back of my tongue. "Cody's got a lot of monsters to kill," she said, "if you want to help me make an arsenal."

I RETURNED TO Talcum as a man. Or beneath the skin of a man. After five years alone in Maine, I felt feral and directionless, despite the transition. My mother helped me get a little apartment near the university, and I enrolled in a few basic courses to see if I could straighten myself up and figure out a future. The university, so dinky that most of the professors were retired high school teachers with state pensions, had only recently been upgraded from a two-year college designation.

I worked weekends at a family-owned shop called Danny Hernandez Printing. The warehouse where I spent most of my time was a weird little honeycomb of rooms full of stacks of disorganized papers and decade-old machinery. The weekend staff was just me and a river rat named Joey, who worked weekends at Danny Hernandez so he could finance the rest of his life on the banks of the Comal.

Our jobs were deeply boring. The copy machines at Danny Hernandez were ancient and temperamental, designed for paper-to-paper copies only. Joey and I spent most of our time trying to create perfect hard copy originals from imperfect Photoshop printouts, or squinting at illegible handwritten directions. The front of the shop was full of office supplies and stuffed animals, printer ink and greeting cards. When I applied, I thought I would be working in the store-front, straightening and stocking, helping customers find just the right alphabet stickers for birthday banners.

A few days after stopping by Sherman House, I skipped my Friday afternoon English class and drove to Our Lady of Guadalupe to sit in the parking lot. I'd printed a banner at Danny Hernandez the weekend before, so I knew the time, date, and plate price for Cody's Barbeque fundraiser. That afternoon was cool enough to wear a jacket; the cold front promised to us the week before finally blew in. I put the card to Cody in my pocket so I could return it to the porch on one of my stalking circuits. The gibbous moon was out, faint but insistent, behind wisps of high clouds. I parked under a live oak and waited.

After about half an hour, a hundred people had gone into the parish hall. Only a few were taking their orders to go, so I pulled my collar up, tucked my chin, and went in. The line was long, the smell of brisket and bodies and floor cleaner overpowering.

I got in line behind Father Declan, a grizzled Irish guy with a cough. He spoke brightly to a young couple with a baby while his hands troubled the top of his belt. I paid the woman behind the cash register and she handed me a Styrofoam plate. As the priest beside me pondered aloud the caloric difference between the mustard potato salad and the mayonnaise, I heard Jill's voice in the kitchen behind the serving window. I hadn't seen her since the summer after our senior year of high school, and back there among the stacks of foil barbeque pans she seemed smaller but sharper, the way my old bedroom did the day I returned from Maine.

I didn't hear anything else from the priest's mouth, even though I was pretty sure his potato salad questions were pointed at me. Instead, I took a long look at the side of Jill's face and dumped my empty Styrofoam box into a trash can on my way out the door. I waited outside an hour before she appeared.

Like everyone else who knew me from before, she let her eyes travel the length of my body before she stopped. It wasn't a smile, exactly, that she offered, but there wasn't anything terrible behind her eyes. The sidewalk was uncomfortably busy.

Jill reached for my face. "Turn your head," she said, flattening the palm of her hand against my cheek. It was not a tender gesture. "I recognized you," she told me. "Not your face, at first, but there was something." She stopped. "Your hands, maybe." She dropped her fingers and picked up my thumb, examining the knuckles of my left hand. The thing I remembered most when I thought about her in the intervening years was her hair—fine spikes that drooped like sunflower stalks at the end of the day. Her hair was a dark streaky blonde now, cut into an inoffensive queer fade.

I didn't believe that she recognized my hands, but flexed my fingers and looked at them with her. They hadn't changed much. It occurred to me that she was touching me openly in the street, something she'd never have done in high school when I was recognizable as a girl.

"What are you doing here?" she asked.

I shrugged. "I'm taking some classes over at the college. The *university*."

Jill squinted past me, down the street. "This place hasn't changed a bit."

I turned around, following her gaze. Mueller's Ice House had burned a few months back, taking with it the back of Friedeck's Hardware and a little exotic animal store that sold crickets you could feed to your pet lizard. The signs were still there; the brick facades had been left pretty much untouched. I didn't tell her that the insides of the stores had melted.

"How's Cody?"

Jill stuck her hands into her back pockets and shrugged. "Still breathing."

We hadn't talked since the week before she left for Smith—when she'd unceremoniously broken up with me in the courtyard. I'd agreed with her that the first relationship never lasts, and that we should both try to have sex with as many people as possible in the coming years—that it was wasteful to be so young and so tied to one person. I could only agree and couldn't bring myself to mention the actual reasons we could no longer look each other in the face.

"I thought you might be back," I said. "I just wanted to talk to you again. See how you're doing."

"Well, your timing is terrific, here on the street under the watchful gaze of the Virgin. You could have sent a card or something first." Jill finally met my eyes straight on, as though she were no longer afraid of what she might see. "What am I supposed to call you now?" She asked.

"Emmett," I said.

"Your mom call you that?"

"When she remembers." My mother had actually been the least of my worries. She recognized pretty immediately that my safety in Talcum depended on the disappearance of her daughter and the sudden appearance of a nephew with her maiden name. I think, after the shock and disappointment, she was just glad to have me around again.

Jill turned to wave at a car inching past. I recognized her mother in the driver's seat.

"You need to go?" I asked.

She sighed as her mother pulled away. "Let's walk," she said, pulling a pack of cigarettes from her messenger bag. "What are you studying, Emmett?"

"Nothing," I said. "I mean, I don't know. Undecided." I took the lit cigarette she handed me and looked around for a less conspicuous place to smoke. I'd told my Mom I'd quit, and Talcum was small. The filter carried the damp scent of Jill, gone the instant I inhaled. I looked at her bag, her shoes, her glasses.

"This time of year means, I'm guessing, you're knee-deep in GMAT prep?"

"Only GRE."

"Married to an activist?"

"Somewhat."

"Somewhat married?" The ring she wore looked hand-crafted.

Jill stooped to pick up a local paper on the corner instead of answering my question. Cody's fundraiser had made the front page. "Must be another slow news day," she said. I asked her how long she'd be in town.

"Depends," she said, and cupped her hands around her eyes to peer into the dark window of Mueller's Ice House. "Fucking hell," she said. "Did you know about this?"

"It's a few months gone now," I said.

"I can't believe this place." When she turned back to me, there was a trenchant anger in her eyes. "And now this. You! You're not supposed to be here."

"Can I see him?"

"If you're looking to make up for past mistakes, now's not the time."

This struck me as unusually cruel. I told her so, crushing the half-smoked cigarette beneath my shoe.

CODY DIDN'T HAVE a lot of success with killing off his monsters his first fall in Talcum, despite our help. He began to venture around his middle school on bathroom breaks, leaving campus altogether if he felt too afraid to return to class. Sometimes he wandered all the way to the high school to wait for our last bell to ring, and then he'd walk home between us. He seemed undisturbed by the chaos his absence created, and shrugged away our concerns.

"You can't get lost in this town," he told Jill. "What's the problem?"

"The problem is that you are going to get yourself kicked out of school," Jill said, her arm around his shoulders.

"You don't know what it's like. I can't be there."

"Isn't there a counselor at school you can talk to?" I asked. Cody ignored my question.

"Cody," Jill said. "Emily wants to know if you can talk to a counselor?"

"No," Cody said, looking at the road directly in front of his feet.

"Why not?"

"He's not family," he said, finally.

Cody's teachers called a meeting after the winter break to set expectations for the new year, so we sat with Cody in the kitchen, drawing weapons and sipping hot chocolate, until his parents returned from school. His monsters that night were in armies of red and black. They required nail bombs and tear gas to set them running.

His mother returned from the meeting, her eyes red-rimmed and puffy, and ushered Cody out the door for pizza, leaving Jill and me alone in the empty house. Once we heard them pull out of the driveway, Jill motioned for me to follow her upstairs into the guest quarters—normally forbidden territory.

"Nobody's here," Jill insisted when she saw me hesitate.

"I need some help with chemistry," I said. "Can we do that first?"

"It'll take a tiny minute. I want to show you something." I followed her up the stairs. The doors on the landing were all closed, numbers burned eye-level into the wood. "Pick a door," she said.

"What is this?" I asked. "I don't want to get in trouble with your parents."

"We have a couple of hours before they get home. I've had these disappointment talks with them before. They think pizza makes it better."

I felt the tingle at the top of my head again, that faint nausea. Jill crossed her arms and lowered her eyes, waiting for me to comply. I stepped forward and turned the tarnished knob of Room 3, palms suddenly a little sweaty. Jill reached past me and flipped the switch on a lamp by the door, illuminating a tiny room crammed with antiques and covered floor to ceiling in green and yellow gingham.

"This is terrible," I said, eyes watering at an overwhelming bouquet of potpourri. Jill stepped inside and closed the door behind us.

"Too late. You chose this place." She brought a hand to her nose and made a face.

"I really thought your mom had better taste."

"All the rooms are different," Jill said, drawing a fat bundle of twigs from a small pouch. She lit the twigs and put them in a little dish on the window sill. "It might be dumb, but I read about something in a book and I want to try it with you." She looked up nervously from the window and sat down cross-legged on the bed. The twigs glowed smokily across the room, a smell of sage pleasantly cutting through the potpourri. I climbed up and sat facing her, closer than I'd ever been to her body without touching it. The tingling at the crown of my head began to make its way down my spine and into my limbs. I knew I would do it, whatever she wanted.

Jill was quiet for a moment, eyes sunken and uncertain, as though reconsidering. Her right knee, millimeters from my left knee, radiated heat.

"Okay, I'm going to look at you. You're going to look at me." She rested her hands, palm upward, on her knees. I did the same.

"Don't we do that every day?"

"Not like this. Sustained eye contact. It's different. You'll see."

"And why couldn't we do this downstairs?"

"That's their space. You chose this room, I lit the sage. That makes this is *our* space." Jill took a deep breath and closed her eyes. I took a deep breath and closed my eyes. "At the count of three," she whispered, "open your eyes and look at me."

When I did, when she did, when I quit laughing and when she quit telling me to shut up, everything but her pupils, everything in my periphery, covered over in gold sheeting and pulsed so slowly I couldn't keep track of my own breath. We sat that way until driveway headlights ribboned across the room and broke the connection. She was right. It was different.

That night I dreamed of her looking down at me from her closet window, her face visible behind the stained glass. I stood in the courtyard, cloaked in longing. I didn't know what I longed for, really. At seventeen, my erotic thoughts were confined to the impossible relationships of Harold and Maude, Mrs. Robinson and Ben, Atreyu and the Childlike Empress. I understood that shadowy possibilities existed between the two of us. I understood, too, that we should not talk about them.

One damp spring night Cody finished his work on the floor and climbed onto the loveseat, leaning wordlessly against my arm. He fished his Gameboy out of his hoodie pocket and began a game of Mario Cart. I'd never been so close to him. Jill returned from the kitchen with a plate of cookies. She set them silently on the coffee table in front of us and then sat down on the other end of the loveseat. Over his head, she gave me a thumbs-up before pointing the remote at the television.

I continued to dream of Jill in the window; her image there etched so finely that I could barely look her in the eyes until we were in Room Three, sage alight on the windowsill. Soon after, I quit the newspaper because our late production nights were Wednesday and Thursdays. I was set for a chance to make editor my senior year, and had to work to convince myself that I didn't care.

Too AGITATED TO go home after the sidewalk reunion with Jill, I stopped at a convenient store for some gum. I hadn't smoked since top surgery, and a sick, sour taste had risen in the back of my throat. Next door at Talcum Treasures, I picked up some flowers.

Cody's hospital room walls were painted a lovely shade of indigo. His blinds were open, slate northern light settling over the side of his face left un-bandaged. I put my tulips on his bedside table, next to three other arrangements. Somebody was dreaming of this boy, of his bullet-shattering futures. I sat down and examined the forearm I'd once found so dismaying. He was no longer an adolescent, but retained a familiar spray of freckles across his nose and cheek. He probably wouldn't wake up this time.

I wondered if Cody's altar on the front porch of Sherman House annoyed Jill. Probably it did, but all the same, I wished there could be a place like it for the living. A place to build an altar to the ones who are not yet gone, and to the ones who will one day leave. A public place for the most private of memories, of pictures, of shameful prayers for possession.

When I got out of Talcum, I found a way to avenge the ravage of puberty and beat my own mind at its mirror tricks. I went as far north as I could manage. I'd manifested. My new shoulders, my scars. My hips, wrested from their child-bearing future. I'd pulled my insides to the surface and could now shave my face like any other man. Most of the guys in my therapy group found some kind of peace in their new bodies—even relief. They recorded milestones in journals and took strings of self-portraits, which they posted online and shared with family members.

What I found was not so much peace as a new kind of understanding of what my body was not. It would never grow three inches in a summer. It would never fit into straight-legged jeans or shirts straight off the rack. It would never unconsciously enter a room of people and feel like it wasn't hiding some eternal truth. It was not a body Jill would ever love again, or anything I could explain. By vanishing my own past for the chance to see a future, a big part of what I'd manifested was loss.

THE SUMMER BETWEEN my junior and senior year, Jill and Cody were sent back to Boston to make the rounds of relatives they'd left behind. She sent one postcard with a picture of a beach on the front: Cody seemed happier, she was bored, they went to a baseball game with old friends and ate lobster rolls on the cape.

Because I'd ditched every other friend I'd ever had to spend all my time with Jill, I passed the summer in a liminal space between waking and sleeping, drifting from memory into headphones, unable to hold sustained conversations with anyone.

There was only the one postcard from Boston that entire summer. My mother worked double shifts when she could, worrying at me in the kitchen while we fixed toast and bacon. She agreed to sign me up for Driver's Ed if I'd find a job during the school year to pay her back, and by the end of the summer I had my license. I don't remember anything about that class, but somewhere along the way that summer

I must have developed enough muscle memory to pass the road test. I wrote to Jill most afternoons and dropped the letters at Sherman House for her parents to mail.

I avoided revealing the true depth of my despair in the letters. It wasn't just the loneliness. It was my body, which seemed to be deciding my future without consent. Mornings often brought unwelcome surprises—my period a week early, a long purple stretch mark down my left thigh, a painful crop of forehead acne. I put on weight though my diet hadn't changed much and grew out of my sports bras and jeans before the end of July. When I felt consumed by grief, I'd drive by Sherman House and try to conjure the sage, golden overlay and the lightness of limb after three or eight minutes of Jill's attention.

My mother was pleasantly surprised that I hadn't taken after the women on her side of the family, who were slim and wiry. She took me thrifting for summer clothes, saying we should save our money for the fall, given my rate of growth. "In a few years you'll be happy about those hips," she said, waving off my concern. "I thought you and your big newborn head were going to do me permanent damage." I managed to leave the store with a few pieces that hid my hips and new C cups well enough, but soon learned to artfully avoid catching my reflection in mirrors or shop windows. I got a job at the Dairy Queen down the street from Sherman House and though we were allowed to make ourselves a free shake after each shift, I refused to give my body any more incentive to continue its betrayal. When I thought about my future, I saw a stranger in my place.

———————

JILL SHOWED UP on my doorstep a few days before school started, golden-skinned and three months taller. Her hair was boy-short.

"Nobody offered to take you in up north?" I asked, going for a lightness that wasn't really in me.

"Who could leave beautiful Talcum behind?" Jill sounded fake, too.

"I volunteer!" I rose my hand, and my old t-shirt rose to expose skin above my hips.

"I brought you something," she said, pressing a little bag into my hand. "Come over later? They're taking Cody to a new therapist in San Antonio tonight, and then out to a movie." She let herself out, calling goodbye to my mother from the door. I opened the bag and found a braided leather bracelet with a number three pressed into the top of the silver clasp.

Cody returned to Texas taller than both Jill and me. He'd cut his hair back from his face and sprouted cheekbones over the course of the summer. Slim, muscled, and newly graceful in his gait, there was a reserved sort of confidence in his eyes. Jill was right. He looked happier. The three of us returned to the loveseat on the back porch as though no time had passed, but we were all a little bigger, the couch a little smaller. Cody let his body unfold between us. I asked him about Boston and he spoke at length about the Red Sox from behind his Game Boy.

Jill and I snuck into to Room 3 that night after everyone was asleep. The middle of the week was a good bet for privacy, and there were no guests. I'd thought about being back in Room 3 so often over the summer that the climb upstairs was dream-like and full of portent. Something dangerous and quivering settled into my chest on the landing.

While we held eye contact, I could feel something rising to the surface of my skin, molecules rearranging. She leaned in, not breaking contact; I leaned back a shade, not believing I could trust the room wasn't simply tilting us into a new parallel plane. It was all brain chemicals. I know that now. But that night, my senses opened like morning glories to the dawn. The sound of her eyelashes coming together, her lips parting, the steady rhythm of lungs beneath my palm. As her warm hand made contact with the skin I'd accidentally exposed that morning, it occurred to me that maybe she was a little less disappointed by my summer body than I was.

CODY MADE PROGRESS with his new therapist, Irving. He ditched his jeans and tent-like shirts in favor of athletic shorts and Astros jerseys, though I'd never seen him touch a baseball. He told us he made a friend at school, someone named Ali from his math class. The most we knew about that was that his math teacher hadn't reported any unexcused absences. He still fell asleep on the floor of Jill's room, but we could wake him up and guide him to his own room without too much trouble. The house felt oxygenated, less trussed.

Jill and I spent the fall working on college applications, and had our packets and essays in the mail by December. We proofed one another's essays and complicated forms that had to be filled out in ink. Jill helped me apply to a few state universities within an hour's drive; my mother could help me out with a place to live if I could cover my own tuition. I helped Jill apply all over the country, mostly small east coast schools that encouraged students to make up their own degree plans. I flipped through her college information catalogs while she debated the merits of professors' publications. Then I tried to wipe the images of snow-covered libraries and wooded mountain passes from my mind while her fingers unbuttoned my shirt and pushed me gently onto the bed in Room 3. Every third Wednesday, Jill went to see Irving with Cody. One of those nights I swiped a few of the catalogs from her pile of castoffs and tried, from my room at home, to imagine myself tucked into a dorm at a girls' school on a New Hampshire hill. I knew it was impossible, with mediocre grades and no extra-curriculars, to count on a scholarship.

I kept working weekends. Through the warm winter holidays and a cold February, we waited for Wednesdays, waited for word from universities, waited for Cody to draw another set of monsters. Evenings, we circled Talcum in my mother's car, listening to music and following backroads that led nowhere. My DQ coworker Shay served us the free end-of-shift blizzards I'd refused for months. Strangers in line complimented Cody's height and beauty. Shay slipped him her number and then took it back when Jill told her he was in eighth grade.

I found his new lean, subtle muscles beneath his jerseys distracting.

Sometimes he'd curl up next to me on the love seat, and I'd unconsciously recoil from the touch of his skin. He was heavier now, in both weight and scent, and clammy from whatever weather he'd run in from. The sweat just above his lip beaded on fine mustache hairs that made me angry in a way I couldn't quite explain.

"He wants to play baseball next year," Jill told me one Wednesday night, her bare thigh resting comfortably against mine on the rug of Room 3.

"Has he ever played?"

"We're just happy he wants to do something other than hide on the back porch."

"They'll laugh him off the field if he's never played before. It's a serious game here."

"Can't you coach him a little? See if he has potential?" I'd aged out of girls' little league at fourteen, and there was no high school softball for girls.

"I guess, assuming I'll be around." We hadn't talked about anything past graduation, given the uncertainty of the next few months, and the thought of throwing a ball with Cody at the park all summer filled made me feel prickly.

"Where else would you be?" Jill asked, checking her watch and rolling away toward our pile of clothes. "It's getting late."

"Maybe I applied a few places you don't know about." I wanted the words to sound intriguing, but they came out mean. One hopeless night in January, I'd thrown together an application for one of the schools from that pile of swiped catalogs: a long shot in Maine that would put me a reasonable bus ride away from any one of her preferred universities.

Jill slipped one arm through her flannel and faced me, confused. "What? Where?"

Before I could answer, there was a shout from downstairs. Jill threw my clothes at me and pulled on her jeans.

"I'm not going to hang around here for the rest of my life, waiting for you to come home for Thanksgiving or whatever," I said.

"Okay," Jill said. "Put your shirt on." Another shout: Cody was in the kitchen, then on the stairs. Jill kicked her shoes under the bed and slipped out the door, pulling it shut behind her. I don't think her pants were buttoned. I tiptoed behind the bed and dressed quietly.

"Where are Mom and Dad?" Jill asked.

"Groceries. It's gonna be full this weekend. What are you doing?"

"Nothing," Jill said.

"Lie. Is Em in there? I want to ask her something."

"She went home an hour ago. Go downstairs and call her." I heard Cody retreat. Jill waited a couple of seconds to make sure he was gone and softly turned the knob again.

I stood on the other side of the bed while she dug around under the bed for her shoes. "I don't expect you to wait around for me. I just thought—" she sat down on the bed to tie her laces. "He's finally doing better. When I leave for school, I figured you'd stick around."

"For him?"

"Yeah," Jill said. "He trusts you." She stood and straightened the bedcovers. "Let's get you out the back before he figures out you're here."

"Zip your pants," I said, not moving. "Hey Cody!" I called. He came bounding up the stairs again. This time, he came through the door himself and stood there, a little stunned at the sight of me in Room 3. He paused a moment.

"I knew you were lying," he said to Jill before turning to me. "I wanted to tell you that Irving wants to meet you. Next Wednesday."

"Why does Irving care about me?" I asked.

Cody shrugged. "I've been talking about you. He's got this big dog named Larry who sits on the couch next to you if you want. It's very comforting."

Jill crossed her arms and looked out the window. I knew I should say yes. I knew I should want to. "I'm not your family," I said.

WHEN THE REJECTION from St. Anselm College in Maine appeared in my mailbox, Jill and I hadn't spoken in two weeks. One of those weeks was spring break. Before she and Cody left for the cape, Jill called and left a message saying she'd be gone and that we should talk when she returned. I asked for more hours at DQ, and my mother dropped me off there each day before her own shift at the Sizzler. She brought home an international cookbook from the library and proposed that we eat like world travelers all week. We took turns making meals for each other, substituting ingredients we didn't have for ones we did, which mostly worked. I didn't call Jill.

The Wednesday night after spring break, I got a call at work and my mother showed up a few minutes later to drive me to the ER. She waited with me for a few hours until Jill and her mother emerged to tell us that Cody was being moved to a psychiatric hospital in San Antonio, but that he would be fine. While our mothers spoke quietly by check-in, I put a few dollar bills in Jill's hand and walked her to the vending machines.

"He was fine in Boston," she said. The blue light from the Pepsi machine made bruises of the skin around her eyes. "Just normal."

"Is he awake now?"

"He's saying he didn't mean it. They pumped his stomach."

"He just doesn't want to go to San Antonio. Leave you." I said.

"Right. Of course he meant it. You can't take a whole bottle of aspirin accidentally."

"Why today? Today's Irving."

"I got into Smith," she told me. "He found the envelope." Jill smoothed a dollar bill and tried, unsuccessfully, to get it lined up with the slot in the machine. I put the money in myself and she leaned against the Big Red button so hard the whole machine tilted backward.

"Come on. That's not why," I said. Jill gave a kind of one-shouldered shrug that meant she didn't believe me.

"Have you slept?"

"I have not," she said, offering me the first sip from her can. I dug my change out of the coin return and bought another drink. "You feel like coming over tomorrow? After we get him settled at the hospital?"

"I have to work," I said, though Shay had offered to trade mid-week shifts with me when I told her about Cody. I did want to come over. I also wished she had already left for the north again. I couldn't figure out what to say next.

I WAS STILL sitting at Cody's bedside when Jill returned to the hospital. I noticed her ring finger was bare of the flat silver band she'd worn earlier. When I'd lived in Maine for those first few years, visiting my mom had always fostered in me the urge to stop wearing shoes and drop my clothes all over the floor. It didn't feel regressive, quite. More like shrugging off a heavy jacket on a too-warm day. Maybe she'd shed her ring like that.

Jill sat down and took my hand. Cody's IV clicked on. "What if we skipped all the boring shit about your transition and my obvious women's studies concentration?

"I'm okay with that," I said. "Anyway, from what I understand, transition's now part of the Smith curriculum."

"He's been okay for a while now," Jill said. "He's going to graduate this spring. Last year was a bit rough so I invited him to visit, to get outside this shithole, and Mom and Dad wouldn't let him come."

"Are they upset you're queer?" I asked.

"No, they're okay with Susan. They were just too scared to let him out of their sight for five minutes."

"Her name is *Susan*?"

"So?"

"Nothing. Where's your ring?"

Jill tightened her grip on my hand just a bit. "Were you a really a boy when I met you?"

"I don't know. But it's important to me that you knew me before,"

I said, finally. The transition cuts a life in half, I told her. I moved freely finally, in a skin I could believe, the kind of skin I'd envied in her brother. But the new skin erased my past, unburdened my future. I was a different person with everybody. I sometimes claimed a panicked false past for the sake of smoothing over a misunderstanding. Or I came out so I wouldn't have to think about it, and then that's all I was. But with her, I was backlit.

"I was in Maine the whole time," I said.

"Your mom told me. I went looking for you that first Thanksgiving."

"I couldn't stay."

"I know."

I dug the red envelope out of my bag and handed it to her. "Somebody really loves Cody," I said.

"We all love Cody," Jill said. The sun was almost gone, and the bare tree limbs in the parking lot of the hospital were black against a purpling sky. "I hope it's enough."

Acknowledgements

WITH THANKS TO: S. Kirk Walsh for her essential guidance as a teacher, writer, and editor; Paige Schilt, who not only introduced me to Trystan Cotten at Transgress, but also answered every question and offered endless, cheerful advice; Trystan Cotten and everyone at Transgress who worked to get this book out into the world; Susan Post at Bookwoman, who provides an invaluable space to envision a bright future for trans, queer, feminist writers everywhere; Erin Pringle and Robin Storey, who read, edited, and championed early versions of these stories; My family of writers - Abby Nance, Carmen Edington, Michael Wolfe, Amelia Gray, Tim Kerlin, Sara Faulkner, John Dean, and Rene Perez, who named this book; The Kirkshop and Austin Writer's Lab; Adriana Rangel, for the haunted, beautiful cover; Julie Wernersbach, Michael Noll, Stephen Bottum for early encouragement; Sue, David, and Bennie Kaulfus for their never-ending and uncomplicated support; and Bianca Garza, who believes in the bookstore church and never minds writing hours as long as the door between us is always open.

ALSO PUBLISHED BY TRANSGRESS PRESS

Swimming Upstream: A Novel
Jacob Anderson-Minshall

Trans Homo…Gasp!
Gay FTM and Cisgender Men on Sex and Love
Avi Ben -Zeev and Pete Bailey

Lou Sullivan
Daring To Be A Man Among Men
Brice D. Smith

Trunky (Transgender Junky)
A Memoir of Institutionalization and Southern Hospitality
(Lambda Literary Finalist 2016)
Sam Petersoon

Life Beyond My Body
Transgender Journey to Manhood in China
(Lambda Literary 2016)
Lei Ming

Words of Fire!
Women Loving Women in Latin America
Antonia Amprino

The Wanderings of Chela Coatlicue
Touring Califaztlan
Ananda Esteva

Queer Rock Love: A Family Memoir
Paige Schilt

I Know Who You Are, But What Am I?
A Partner's Memoir of Transgender Love
Ali Sands

Love Always
Partners of Trans People on Intimacy, Challenge, and Resilience
Edited by Jordon Johnson and Becky Garrison

Real Talk for Teens:
Jump-Start Guide to Gender Transitioning and Beyond
Seth Jamison Rainess

Now What?
A Handbook for Families with Transgender Children
Rex Butt

New Girl Blues...or Pinks
Mary Degroat Ross

Letters for My Sisters: Transitional Wisdom in Retrospect
Edited by Andrea James and Deanne Thornton

Manning Up: Transsexual Men on
Finding Brotherhood, Family and Themselves
Edited by Zander Keig and Mitch Kellaway

Hung Jury: Testimonies of Genital Surgery by Transsexual Men
Edited by Trystan Theosophus Cotten

Below the Belt: Genital Talk by Men of Trans Experience
Edited by Trystan Theosophus Cotten

Giving It Raw: Nearly 30 Years with AIDS
Francisco Ibañez-Carrasco